I0788207

CRAIG HALLORAN

Dragon Wars: Grey Cloak - Book 13

By Craig Halloran

Copyright © 2020 by Craig Halloran

Amazon Edition

TWO-TEN BOOK PRESS

PO Box 4215, Charleston, WV 25364

ISBN eBook: 978-1-946218-90-2

ISBN Paperback: 979-8-580671-67-3

ISBN Hardback: 978-1-946218-89-6

WWW.DRAGONWARSBOOKS.COM

Publisher's Note

This book is a work of fiction. Names, characters, places, and incidents either are the product of the author's imagination or are used fictitiously, and any resemblance to actual persons, living or dead, events, or locales is entirely coincidental.

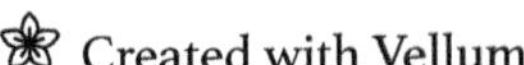 Created with Vellum

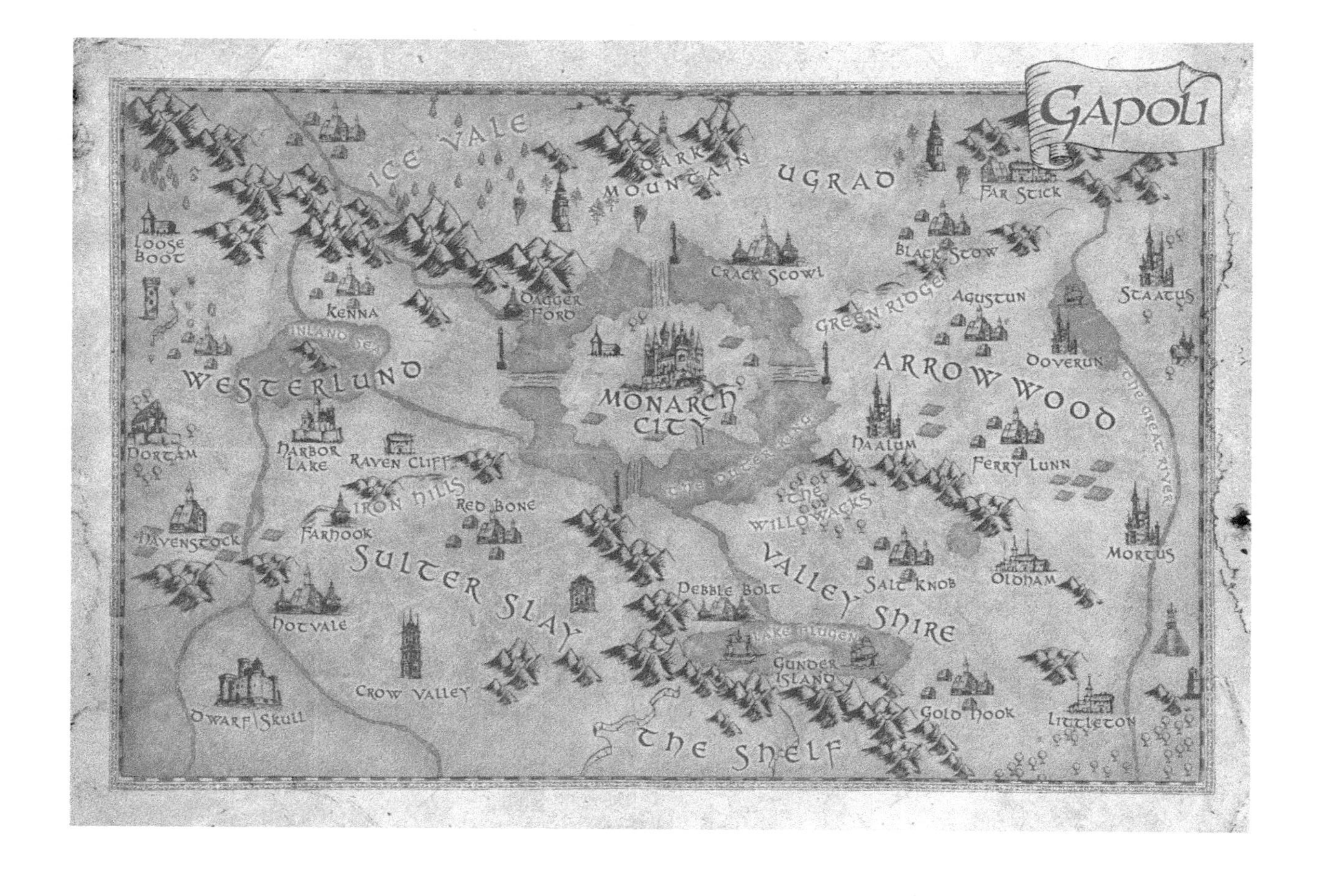

Gadoli
ICE VALE
DARK MOUNTAIN
UGRAD
FAR STICK
LOOSE BOOT
CRACK SCOWL
BLACK STOW
STAATUS
KENNA
DAGGER FORD
GREEN RIDGE
AGUSTUN
DOVERUN
WESTERLUND
ARROW WOOD
MONARCH CITY
DORTAM
HARBOR LAKE
RAVEN CLIFF
NAALUM
FERRY LUNN
THE OUTER RING
THE GREAT RIVER
IRON HILLS
RED BONE
WILLO WACKS
HAVENSTOCK
FARHOOK
SULTER SLAY
VALLEY SHIRE
MORTUS
DEBBLE BOLT
SALT KNOB
OLDHAM
HOTVALE
LAKE FLUGEN
GUNDER ISLAND
DWARF SKULL
CROW VALLEY
GOLD HOOK
LITTLETON
THE SHELF

1

BISH

Using his muscular arms and hands like tools, Venir snapped the broken-off table legs in half then chucked them into the fireplace. The huge black cat lying on the hearth hissed at him but didn't budge an inch.

"What are you fussing at, Octopus?" Venir asked in a gusty voice. "Those flames will keep your mangy fur warm." He swung his iron gaze toward the bar and found Sam, the barkeep, glaring at him. "Don't worry, Sam. I'll pay for the table. Put it on my tab."

Sam slung his dish towel over his shoulder and shook his head. "Stop doing swan dives on my tables. The next time you do it, you're out of here."

Venir smiled. "You said that the last time."

"Don't try me." Sam walked through the double doors that led back into the kitchen.

The moment Venir's hard stare caught Tatiana's eyes, goose bumps popped up on her arms. The massive man, bare-chested and all muscle, came right toward her.

His speech was slurred a little when he closed one eye and spoke. "I know you."

Her body was pressed between him and the bar as he mimed swallowing her whole. "Yes, we've met."

"I've never seen eyes like yours. Eyes that I'll never forget." He gently tucked her hair behind one pointed ear with a calloused hand. "Those are cute." He ran his gaze all over her body. "But you are not as full-figured as before. You are fragile. Are you ill?"

Erin, a young warrior woman, tapped Venir hard on the shoulder and matter-of-factly said, "She's fine." The well-built blonde had a strong resemblance to her father. Her shoulders were broad, and her limbs were sinewy like Venir's. She wore her weather gear and sword belt like a seasoned soldier. "Can you tear your eyes away from this wanderer and say hello to your daughter?"

"Eh?" Venir's face met his child's. "Erin!" He picked her up underneath her armpits and spun her around like a little girl. He wrapped his bulging arms around her in a massive bear hug that would have broken the back of an ordinary woman. "What are you doing here?"

"Looking for you." Erin slipped away from his strong arms with a sour face. "You sweat like a hog and reek of their flesh."

"That's the man in me!" he boasted. "Sam, a tankard for me and my daughter! And one for our acquaintance."

"No, thank you," Tatiana said as she stared at her goblet of sour wine. "I've had my fill."

Venir took a new tankard in hand and guzzled half of it down. Foam ran into his beard, and he wiped it off with his hand. He looked between the two frowning women and said, "How did the pair of you meet?"

Erin grabbed his shoulders and turned him toward her. "Mother sent me to bring you home."

"Kam did that? Why? She knows that I'm in Bone. I told her I'd return after a month well spent."

The lioness of a woman crossed her arms. "Yes, you did. Over six months ago."

"Oh." Venir scratched the short blond hair on his nearly bald head. "Tell her I'll return shortly. But tonight, we live!" He hoisted his tankard high in the air and chanted, "For Bone! For Bone! For Bone!"

A few of the tavern dwellers responded with half-hearted effort.

Venir gave them a disappointed look and said to Tatiana, "It's still early. They'll wind up in a few more hours. Let's find a table, shall we? I'm curious why you're here, eh... what is your name? I never had the pleasure."

"Tatiana."

He took her hand and Erin's, led them to a table, and

sat. "It's good to be with family and old, well, acquaintances. How did the pair of you meet?"

"We met moments before you belly flopped on the table." Erin sucked down half of her tankard then banged it on the bar. "Father, you need to return. Mother worries. And I'm not leaving without you."

Venir knitted his eyebrows together for a moment. His mirthful demeanor vanished, and a melancholy mood took over. "I hate that anyone worries about me," he mumbled. With a shake of his head, he focused his attention on Tatiana. "But why are you here? When I saw you before, I was young, and the moment was but a dream, but now you appear real?"

"It's a long story, but I was seeking you out. Mood told me to find you," she said as she fanned herself. "Elf stones, it's hot in here. And you have a fire going." Her robes clung to her body. "How do you stand it?"

Venir and Erin shrugged.

"This is the colder time of the year," Erin said. She took out a dagger and flipped it over her hand. "Without the fire, my bones would chill."

Venir leaned his chair back onto two legs. "Mood sent you to me?" He rubbed his noggin with his fingers. "Why?"

"I'm not from this world. I come from another. Invaders from your world have poisoned my own. They sent me here." She absentmindedly sipped her warm wine then nearly spit it out. "Lords of Thunder, that's awful."

A slender man set a chair down between Tatiana and Erin. "Perhaps I can finish it for you." He easily wedged himself between them and offered Tatiana a handsome smile. "Allow me to introduce myself, beautiful. I am Melegal."

2

———

MELEGAL'S bony fingers were as cold as ice, and Tatiana had trouble slipping her fingers from his viselike grip. Oddly enough, his cool hands were comforting, though, and he let his grip linger. He wore a floppy dark-gray cap that was smooth on one side. His face was slim, with angular features, high cheekbones, and a pointy, dimpled chin. He wore a golden silk shirt under a purple vest, and his steely gaze wouldn't let go of hers.

Finally, she managed to slip free of his grip and glanced at Erin. "Nice to meet you."

"He's one of us," Erin said as she put her dagger away. "But don't believe a word he says. He only gets my father into trouble."

"Me? We all know better than that." Melegal didn't take his eyes away from Tatiana's. "Tell me more about yourself,

Tatiana." He grabbed her hand again. "Your bone structure is wonderful. Please, let me read your palm. I can learn much about a woman that way."

"Yes, ask his wife, Rayal," Erin quipped. "Or perhaps one of his many children. Shouldn't you be tending to matters in the castle?"

Melegal scratched his neck. "Shouldn't you be bearing your own children by now?"

Erin's cheeks reddened. "Don't make me throttle that skinny neck of yours."

Venir chuckled, and he raised his tankard. "Another!"

"You'll have to forgive Erin. She takes after her father and broods," Melegal said to Tatiana, "which means she's not very much fun."

"Oh, stuff your hole. I can drink you under the table any day, you old hag," Erin said.

Melegal raised a brow. "Is that a challenge?"

Erin leaned toward him. "You only want free drinks."

"Those are the best kind." Melegal rubbed his small pot belly, which barely hung over his waistband. "But I'll take your bet."

"Keep me out of it. The last skim we ran didn't turn out so well for me," Venir said as he smoothed his hand over his shaved head. "I never realized my hair carried such value."

Erin gave her father a shocked look. "Is that what happened? You lost your locks in a skim?"

Venir shrugged. "Slat happens."

"Mother will kill you."

Melegal tapped the table with his hand. "Excuse me, little sister, but are we wagering or not?"

"Oh, we are wagering!" Erin bounced a silver coin on the table. "Winner of the toss picks the spirit of their choice."

"I'm in!" Venir said.

"No, you aren't!" Melegal and Erin said at the same time.

Melegal thumbed his chest. "I'm flipping."

"You most certainly are not. You've never lost a coin flip that you tossed in your life," Erin said.

"That's the point," Melegal replied.

"Give me the coin. I'll toss it," Venir said.

Tatiana spread her arms out over the table and said, in a loud voice, "Stop it! Please, stop it! I didn't come here to observe your mindless customs!"

Venir, Erin, and Melegal fell silent.

Venir lowered all four chair legs to the ground. "Pardon us. You said that Mood sent you. That must be important." He rested his forearms on the table. "Please, go on, Tatiana."

"Thank you." Her voice cracked, and she had no choice but to take a drink from her goblet. "I don't know how much time I have. I was sent to this world so that the invaders from your world can return. I can be summoned back at any time."

Venir tilted his head. "Is that what happened to me all those years ago? I was *summoned*?"

"Yes and no. You were brought here with a device called the Figurine of Heroes. It has the power to pull people from other worlds at any point in time. It could be from your past or future, but my world does not have control over it. It's random."

"Is that how you came to be here?" Melegal asked as he coiled a lock of her hair around his finger.

"No, but it played a part in it. My world is called Gapoli. There are towers called the Wizard Watch, and inside one of them is a towering stone archway called the Time Mural. It opens a gate to other worlds. That is how I came to be here. I was sent through the mural as an experiment to see if I can safely return."

Venir nodded. "I know of such things."

Erin looked surprised. "You do?"

"It's a long story."

Melegal pursed his lips. "Tell me, fair one, how do they summon you home? Does a portal open?"

"I don't know." She revealed the jeweled bronze collar on her neck. "But with this device, they can track me."

Melegal quickly covered her exposed neck. "Don't go flashing that around. You'll only get your head cut off."

"Anyway, I arrived here through the Time Mural. Fortunately, I encountered Mood and told him everything. He sent me here. He said you would want to know about this. Perhaps you can help?"

"I don't follow how Mood thinks that I can help. A wizard could, perhaps, but not a warrior like me," he said.

"You said that there were invaders from our world in your world?" Erin asked. "Who are these invaders, and how did they come to your world?"

Tatiana wrung her hands for a moment and took another drink. "It's complicated."

"I can handle it," Melegal said just as Octopus hopped into his lap. He stroked the purring cat's fur. "I think someone is getting jealous."

"The Figurine of Heroes is a deadly device. I despise it. One never knows what creature it will summon, good or bad. The summoning doesn't last long—maybe minutes, not even an hour—and the being will return home."

"Like me?" Venir asked.

"Yes," she answered. "But in this instance, two fiendish men from your world were summoned. They nearly killed all of us. They should have returned to your world, but they were crafty and jettisoned the figurine into the Time Mural. It trapped them safely in our world, as they did not wish to return to theirs—or here, rather." She glanced about. "I can see why. However, as I understand it, I believe they were dead in this world, and now they are brought back to life. And they want to stay alive."

Venir sat up. His wooden chair groaned. His blue eyes started to narrow. "Tell me more about these invaders."

Tatiana nodded. "Mood was familiar with them. He said that you would be too. One had eyes as pure as gold, and the other's are silver."

Octopus's purring stopped.

"They are brothers who call themselves Lord Verbard and Lord Catten."

Venir's blue eyes appeared to catch fire. He rose then smashed his ham-sized fists through the table. "Underlings!"

3

WIZARD WATCH

HOURS PASSED. Grey Cloak stood at the threshold of an archway sealed by a stone made of pure granite. On the other side of the stone were the underlings. Supposedly.

His gaze drifted to Gossamer. The elven wizard clothed in tattered black-and-white checkered robes bit his nails as he paced the floor. Neither had spoken a word since Grey Cloak almost killed the elf he feared might be deceiving him. His battle with the guardians, an awful snake-like monster, and a skeleton of a wizard had nearly cost him, but he prevailed.

He stood by the slab door with the Figurine of Heroes in hand, practicing the arcane words of power:

Osid-ayan-umra-shokrah-ha.

Osid-ayan-umra-shokrah-ha.

Osid-ayan-umra-shokrah-ha.

Grey Cloak didn't fully understand how the figurine worked. In the past, the creatures he summoned would vanish after a short spell of time. He only needed the enchanted words to bring them forth. But he wanted to be sure that he dispelled the underlings permanently, so he practiced.

Once this door opens, they may be gone before I see them.

Gossamer broke the silence. "I'm sure they will open it soon. It's never more than a day or so."

"A day?"

"Or days," Gossamer replied politely.

Grey Cloak shook his head. "You reek of deception."

"I serve the tower. I am not permitted to harm you or any other ally. We need trust, Grey Cloak. You and I." The tattered hem of Gossamer's robes dragged as he approached. He raised his hand, palm up. "Let me have the figurine. If they see you with it, they will be prepared for it."

"How will they see me?" he asked. "Can they see through the rock?" He peered deeply into Gossamer's face. "Or through your eyes?"

"No, but I warn you, the underlings are crafty. Well-prepared for anything."

"They can't stay in there forever, assuming they're behind this slab." He wanted to punch the rock but held his fist back. His best hope was Dalsay, the ghostly wizard who had departed to keep tabs on the underlings, but he'd yet to reappear. And if Dalsay was on the other side, Grey

Cloak had no way of knowing. But the two of them shared a special connection. Dalsay had entered Grey Cloak's body in the Ruins of Thannis, and he'd unleashed power in Grey Cloak that he'd never imagined that he had.

He looked at his palm then summoned blue fire, which danced across his fingers.

If this figurine doesn't work, I'm going to have to kill them myself.

The underling lords, Catten and Verbard, stood over the stone pedestal that controlled the Time Mural with intense looks on their evil faces. The silver-eyed Verbard's shoulders were rounded under his black robes as he adjusted the precious stones in the mouth of the pedestal's basin.

Lord Catten stood across from him, his gold eyes glowing and his robes hovering an inch above the ground. He pointed a sharp black fingernail at the stones and chittered.

Without lifting his eyes, Verbard angrily chittered back.

The evil pair had been working on the Time Mural for hours, trying to summon Tatiana back from what they hoped was their home world.

Unbeknownst to them, Dalsay had been watching the entire time. With his body mostly buried inside the stone walls that made up the chambers, Dalsay observed from above, with little more than his nose fully exposed. From his position behind the underlings' pewter thrones, he had a perfect view of everything between him and the Time Mural.

The image inside the mural was a windy landscape of dust and dirt that baked beneath intense sunlight. There was no sign of Tatiana, only dust devils and tumbleweeds, but the image continued to move slowly across the broken landscape.

Lord Verbard rubbed his jaw. "I'm parched."

"This important event exceeds your petty thirst, brother. Stay focused!" Lord Catten said.

Verbard lifted his deadly gaze and met his brother's. "And yet you dare try my patience. We are close. Or rather, I am close. Let us be prepared to celebrate. The journey home and beyond nears."

"I'm not going to unseal the chamber until this task is finished."

Lord Verbard stepped away from the pedestal and rubbed his eyes. He moved to the thrones, where empty wine bottles sat on the stairs of the dais. He lifted one to his lips and took the last drink. "If I thought it would take this long, I would have moved the entire wine cellar up here." He approached the slab that sealed them inside the room. "I'll summon Gossamer." He pushed up his sleeves. "I'm certain the pathetic fool is near."

Perfect! Dalsay thought. *Grey Cloak should be near, and all of this madness can be over. But if the underlings go, how will Tatiana return? We'll need the underlings to do it.*

As Lord Verbard prepared to open the archway, Dalsay lowered himself into full view and said, "I wouldn't do that if I were you."

4

BISH

Everyone cleared out of the tavern the moment Venir had a fit. Two tables died that night, along with several chairs.

Sam stacked the wreckage by the fire, and Melegal paid him a handful of coins.

Tatiana and Erin also remained, but they moved out of harm's way and took their places on barstools. Octopus returned to his spot on the hearth.

Venir leaned on the fireplace mantel with his forearms resting on the stone. His body trembled from time to time.

"What is happening to him?" Tatiana asked. She'd witnessed the huge warrior's eyes glaze over with rage the moment that she'd mentioned the underlings. She'd never seen the likes of it in a man. She'd nearly fallen out of her chair when it happened.

Melegal sat on the stool on the other side of her. "You

opened an old wound, a wound that we hoped was closed forever."

She sat up and rubbed her trembling hands on her thighs. "I'm sorry. I didn't know. I take it he has issues with the underlings."

"We don't talk about underlings anymore in this world." Erin finished her ale and signaled for another. "Especially around my father."

"And there hasn't been anything to talk about since no one has seen an underling in over a decade."

Tatiana gave Melegal a curious look. "What do you mean?"

"Venir killed them all. And since that day, not one has been seen."

Sam offered Tatiana a hot, damp towel to wipe her face with.

She didn't realize she had been sweating so much. "Thank you. So, you are telling me that all of the underlings in this world are dead? Were they a small race of people?"

"No. They numbered in the tens—if not the hundreds —of thousands," Melegal said. "But we'll never know exactly how many, and we don't want to see them ever again. Not after all they put this world through. They are all gone now, thanks to him."

Despite Venir's brutish, superhuman build, Tatiana found it difficult to believe that he could have single-handedly slain thousands of people. "He defeated a race of wizards?"

"Wizards and warriors. Most of them are warriors with deadly skill. Nasty." Melegal paled. "I need a drink." He tapped the bar with two fingers. "Sam."

"I was young when it all happened," Erin offered as her gaze lingered on her father. "He won't tell me the stories, but the others do. If those underlings are in your world, you need to destroy them before they return to this one. They could destroy everything again."

"But there are only two of them. And if he's slain thousands?" Tatiana said.

"I have personal experience with Verbard and Catten. The likes of them is more than a match for the likes of him. They are supposed to be dead, and it sends chills through me that they somehow live again."

Tatiana rubbed her arms. "It sends chills through me too. I never would have considered that the Figurine of Heroes could also bring harm to other worlds."

Erin wiped her mouth on her leather bracer. "Whatever this figurine you speak of is, you should destroy it before it causes more harm."

"That's what I've been trying to do. But a companion of mine is fond of it. That's what put us in this situation."

"Perhaps you need to rid yourself of this companion," Erin suggested.

"I can't do that. He has to learn to do it on his own. Besides, we can't send the underlings back without it."

Venir turned with a hungry, bloodthirsty look in his eyes. "If they return, me and my axe will be waiting."

"Now he's coming around." Melegal drained half of his goblet. "I know that look in his eyes. He'll want to hunt them again, won't you, Venir?"

Venir dragged a chair across the floor and sat down. "It's what I do."

Erin spoke quietly to Tatiana. "With some, the war never ends. This is the last thing Father needs now. He'd finally begun to come around."

"I am sorry. Truly. The underlings fear being sent back home because, I believe, that means their death. That is why they are trying to master the portal, so they can escape death. If we don't defeat them on our world, I'd be certain they would die again in this world or be displaced in another past or future." She sank her head into the palm of her hand. "Oh, the possibilities."

Melegal rubbed her back. "Speaking of possibilities. If you are going to be stranded here for a spell, I'd be delighted to introduce you to"—he caught Erin glaring at him—"my family."

Tatiana shrugged. "It's possible that I might not ever return. I might need a place to stay in this dingy world."

"It isn't all so horrible," Melegal said. "It offers countless splendors."

Erin made her way over to Venir, stood behind him, and placed her hands on his shoulders. "Father, don't let the past haunt you. That battle is over. This moment will pass. Come home with me. Mother misses you dearly."

Venir huffed. "Dearly. I don't know about that."

"If you ask me, he'd rather dance with the underlings," Melegal said quietly.

Venir spoke up. "What's that?"

"Nothing, you bald-headed lout."

Erin rubbed his shoulders. "Come home."

"Well, the journey would give me time to grow some hair back." He clawed his fingers through his beard. "Even though I'm fond of it being short. No need to tie it down." He nodded and rubbed Erin's hand. "It's settled. We'll leave tomorrow."

5

WIZARD WATCH

DALSAY QUICKLY DREW THE UNDERLINGS' heated stares, and the moment his ghostly robes touched the stones of the floor, they flanked him. "I am Dalsay, a servant of the Wizard Watch. I am only here to observe and assist."

Verbard wrung his hands. "You are an apparition. A spy. Do not attempt to deceive us." His glance caught Dalsay's and locked in.

The moment Dalsay met the underling's stare, his eyes began to burn. A tear ran down his cheek. He closed his eyes and turned away, raising his hands before him. "I admit I am here for my own selfish intentions. Tatiana is a close colleague of mine. I only wish to see her return."

Lord Catten passed his arm through Dalsay's spectral figure. "How long have you been watching us, ghost?"

"On and off since you arrived. For the most part, I have

been in hiding. I wander with no purpose, for my body in this form is useless," he said.

"Pathetic is more like it," Lord Verbard said. "He knows our secrets. We must destroy him."

"You cannot kill that which is already dead. I am merely a shadow of my former self. Please. I only wish the best for my colleague."

The underlings chittered among themselves.

Dalsay bought time. He'd been selfish. If Lord Verbard opened the door, it was possible that the underling menace would be banished. But he couldn't leave Tatiana stranded. He needed her back first. Only then could Grey Cloak strike.

Lord Catten rubbed his cheek. "We have been careless, brother. If this shade has been so close, there is no telling what our enemies know." He moved behind the pedestal and passed his hands over the glinting stones.

The image in the archway shifted, twisted, and changed, revealing the inner chambers and corridors of the Wizard Watch. The picture sped from the lower chambers and raced along the spiraling staircases and sloped tunnels toward the top. The image slowed and hovered. The archway entrance to the Time Mural loomed before them. Grey Cloak and Gossamer were in the picture.

"Deceiver!" Lord Verbard cried out. "But well played." He approached the Time Mural and pointed at the Figurine of Heroes palmed in Grey Cloak's hand. "It's seems that our fate is closer at hand than we thought, brother. What do you propose we do?"

Lord Catten studied the Time Mural. His golden eyes twitched. "There are only two of them. Flesh and blood. Bones and water. We'll send all of the forces we can muster from within and destroy them."

A chill ran down Grey Cloak's spine. The Cloak of Legends rustled. He focused his eyes and stared down the corridor. His gaze ran along the walls, and he spotted a yonder attached to the upper wall. The creepy creature was nothing more than a giant eyeball with wings like a bat and eyes like a spider. It stared him down. He pushed off of the wall. "A friend of yours, Gossamer?"

"What?" Gossamer followed Grey Cloak's stare. "Oh my, no. It's no friend of mine, but I'm afraid the underlings know that we are here."

"I'm sure that's a big surprise." Grey Cloak took a deep breath and placed the figurine back into his inner pocket. "Now what?"

"I fear I don't know. It's the unknown."

Grey Cloak grabbed the Rod of Weapons that was propped up against the wall. He felt the urge to run and hide, but something inside him wouldn't give. He'd come that far. He'd gotten that close. He wasn't going to budge. "If I were an underling, what would I do?" he muttered.

Politely, Gossamer said, "I would send more guardians to destroy us."

"I believe that I would too." Grey Cloak approached the yonder and waved. "Hello, donkey skulls. Do you want to come out and play?" He pointed at the sealed archway then raised his hand in a lifting motion. "Open up. Let's talk."

Gossamer stood beside him and peered at the yonder. "What are you doing?"

"Provoking them."

"I don't think that is wise."

"I don't think it makes a difference." Grey Cloak aimed the Rod of Weapons at the yonder. "Let me try something new."

He summoned the wizardry and fed his power into the rod. The end of the shaft started to glow. A small blue fireball shot out and blasted the yonder. Its leathery wings flapped and wiggled. It dropped from its perch, bounced once, then rolled against the toes of Grey Cloak's boots.

"Impressive."

Grey Cloak blew the wisps of energy from the end of the staff. "It is, isn't it?"

A hollow roar sounded from the bowels of the large tunnel.

"What was that?" Grey Cloak asked as he started to backpedal.

"I have no idea. There are many creatures lurking in the corridors of the Wizard Watch, many of which are new and summoned by the underlings themselves." Gossamer slid behind Grey Cloak's shoulder. "It's days like this that I really miss my cane."

"What happened to your cane?"

"An underling, Verbard, snatched it. It was a device similar to your rod. I could feed my powers through it."

"You still have powers, don't you?"

Gossamer nodded. "Of course. After all, I've been a practitioner for decades."

"Put a cork in it. Something comes."

A familiar sound caught Grey Cloak by the pointed ears. It was the subtle scraping of claws on stone. He'd heard it a thousand times in the Dragon Tunnels, a menacing clicking that turned spines to jelly and sent men fleeing for their lives. But this was different.

Click. Drag. Click. Drag. Click. Drag.

Whatever came sounded as if it was dragging its entire body across the slab stones on the floor.

"It sounds slow," Grey Cloak said. The end of his staff blossomed into a spear. "I can deal with slow."

A dragon's head twice the size of a man's snaked its way out of the corridor on a long serpentine neck. It had a crown of small and sharp horns, and its tongue flicked out from between its jagged teeth. A second head matching the first appeared, followed by another and another. All eight snake eyes focused on the men as its heads coiled back. It pulled its body forward on two powerful front legs until the rest of its great girth filled the tunnel. There would be no escape.

"Gossamer, what is that thing?"

"They call it the fearsome. They call it the fabled. They call it *hydra*."

6

"Boy, those underlings sure like to fight dirty," Grey Cloak said. He tipped his head toward Gossamer. "Are you up for this? You don't look like much of a warrior to me."

Gossamer clutched his fist and rotated it in small circles. White rings of mystic energy flowed up around his arms. "This won't be my first scrap, and I don't plan on making it my last, either."

The hydra stretched out its four heads, opened its mouths, and let out a deafening roar. The monster wasn't huge by any stretch, but its body was as broad as a pair of work horses. Its claws dug into the stones beneath it, causing the rock to crack. It dragged itself forward. Two of its ugly heads struck at Grey Cloak. The other pair of heads went at Gossamer.

Pinned in the archway, with the only exit between them and the hydra, Grey Cloak dashed between the monster's two long necks. He jumped on its shoulders and thrust the Rod of Weapons downward.

The hydra let out a howl. "Raaawwwhrrr!" Both heads twisted around the serpentine neck. Its eyes fastened on Grey Cloak. "Raaawwwhrrr!"

"You felt that, didn't you?" Grey Cloak stabbed the monster again, driving the fiery spearhead deep.

The hydra's heads coiled backward. One head struck like a snake.

Grey Cloak jumped to the side.

The second head lashed out and battered him like a ram. It pinned Grey Cloak between the lip of the tunnel entrance and its body. The first head opened its jaws, revealing sharp and crooked teeth. It attacked again.

"No, you don't!" Grey Cloak stuck the rod into the roof of the hydra's mouth and sent wizard fire coursing through the weapon.

The head lit up with brilliant illumination. The eyes inside its skull burned and smoked. It thrashed about like a wild thing with one head knocking into the other. The pair of heads battled one another, biting and howling like ravenous hounds.

Grey Cloak jumped to safety, landing in front of the sealed archway.

White rings of fire bound the other two heads together. Gossamer faced the monster with his arms outstretched and his fingers massaging the air in intricate patterns. His forehead glistened with sweat as he watched the monster twist and writhe. "It is strong. You need to kill it before my spell breaks."

"Do you have any idea where the heart is?" Grey Cloak asked as he ducked underneath one of the hydra's thrashing heads. He knew plenty about dragons, but the creature was different. The heart could be anywhere in its body. "I could use a reference point."

"It's somewhere inside it."

"That really narrows it down." Grey Cloak twirled the rod and danced away from the hydra's flailing heads. He skipped between the swinging necks and rammed the Rod of Weapons as deep as he could into the monster's breast. He pushed hard and sent the point in deep. "Come on! Die, you dreadful thing. Die!"

The worst ear-splitting sound he had ever heard erupted from the monster's jaws. "*Roooaaarrr!*" All four of its faces turned on him. It wasn't dying.

Grey Cloak wiggled his fingers at it and said, "Uh, hello."

"The figurine is too close for my comfort," Lord Catten said. He stood with his hands over the pedestal, rearranging the stones. "I'm not going to take any chances. We need to summon the woman back now and return home."

Lord Verbard smacked his brother's fingers. "Let me do this! I know what I am doing. You make sure our enemy does not penetrate that door."

The image in the Time Mural started to shift and change. In moments, a hot climate with dirt and dust blowing across a rugged and rocky landscape appeared.

Dalsay carefully watched as the underlings began to fulfill his needs. They were going to summon Tatiana back. Once that happened, he would have to find a way to expose the underlings to the Figurine of Heroes and be rid of them once and for all. He turned his attention to the great slab of stone that sealed them inside the chamber. Grey Cloak and Gossamer were on the other side, battling for their lives. He only hoped they would live long enough to see the underling menace gone. The choice was Dalsay's.

Sacrifices had to be made to save his love, Tatiana. If others perished as a result, he would live with it, though he didn't really live at all.

"I have it, brother. I have it," Lord Verbard said as he seethed with glee. "We need to channel our powers together."

Lord Catten's golden eyes glowed fiery hot. He faced the Time Mural. "Yes, yes, I can see the sands of Bish. I can taste the hot air on my tongue. And the woman. She is there. I smell the jasmine that lingers in her hair. Summon her back, brother. Summon her now. We must execute while the connection is strong! I feel it! I feel it! Grab her now!"

7

BISH

THE DAYS WERE long and the evenings quick in the world of Bish. Tatiana shielded her eyes from the glare of the rising suns. Underneath her wizard robes, she wore attire more fit for the rough country. Her jerkin was made from soft cotton, and the short sleeves showed off her tanned arms. Her mud-red dress was hiked up over her knees, allowing her to ride comfortably. Her weathered fingers had a firm grip on the reins.

"How do you fare, Tatiana?" Venir asked. He led the way north, riding on the back of a massive two-headed dog named Chongo, a dwarven setter that was as big as a bull. The mastiff-like beast's stiff tails switched from side to side, and he walked with an easy gait. "Don't forget to quench your thirst. The days in the Outlands are long and hard."

"I'm well aware," she replied. "Every day is long and hard in this world." She dropped her chin. She'd been stranded in Bish for months, and the prickly world had begun to become her home. Her deep thoughts wandered. *Is Gapoli lost? Are my friends dead?* She was losing hope. Taking Venir's advice, she reached for her water skin then drank deeply. The cool water quenched her thirst, but it did little to ease her mind. "I drank. Are you happy now?"

"I'm always happiest in the Outlands," Venir replied.

Erin led her horse alongside Tatiana. "It's true. There's nothing he loves more than the wild. It's difficult to pull him out of it."

"And I thought it was difficult pulling him out of Bone. I didn't think he'd ever leave that miserable city."

"Well, if you haven't learned by now, *Bish happens,*" Erin said with a smile.

Tatiana swatted a large dragonfly from her face. "You can say that again."

The insect continued to pester her. Its wings buzzed near her ears, switching from one to the other.

"Bone!" She summoned her wizard fire, which erupted from her fingers and turned the insect crispy. "Is everything in this place so irritating? Never mind—I know the answer to that."

"Yes, you should by now, but I don't think it is as awful as you say. I think you've spent too much time with Melegal."

"Perhaps." During her stay, she'd become particularly fond of the wiry rogue, who was full of his own salty charm. He'd welcomed her with open arms into his world, complete with a castle, a beautiful wife, and questionably raised children. His wife, Rayal, a raven-haired beauty, had been nothing short of accommodating. But the comfortable accommodations hadn't lasted long. It seemed that wherever Venir and Melegal went, trouble was soon to follow.

Since Tatiana's arrival, she'd been involved in what her new companions called the Royal Games. The ruling classes of the city of Bone never ceased to be at one another's throats in a power struggle between the houses. There were kidnappings, rescues, skirmishes in the streets, and assassination attempts against Venir, Melegal, and their respective families.

They battled monsters in the sewers and defended their home castle from soldiers from two other castles. Men and women with sorcerous abilities turned buildings into wreckage in attempts to destroy them.

Hounds from hellish kennels pursued them, warriors challenged them, and soldiers chased them.

Tatiana had witnessed it all, battling alongside them. Her senses were on edge. She'd tapped into the world's magic and learned to call it her own. If that was life on Bish, she wasn't sure it was worth living. But she wouldn't quit. Something about her present company made her tougher.

If they can live here, so can I. But home would be far better. "So your mother is a sorceress?" she asked.

"Aye," Erin replied with a prideful smile. "And she's tougher than Father. When he finally returns home, he'll get an earful. I can't wait to see it."

Tatiana stared at Venir's expansive, muscle-laden back. "I find it hard to believe that any woman can handle the likes of him." She'd witnessed Venir butcher swarms of soldiers as if they were sheep. The mere thought of it made her spine quake. "Is she—"

"Burly? Like him? No, Mother is quite a beauty. You'll see."

Tatiana tipped her chin. "Interesting."

"Of course, there might be a funeral before we get after your needs."

"What do you mean?" She eyed Venir. "Oh, I understand the jest. I think I'm getting more familiar with it, but I've never had much of a sense of humor. It would be interesting to see a woman whip your father into shape."

Erin laughed. "Oh, it will be interesting."

"I can hear you," Venir said. "You sound like a couple of gossiping hags."

"Hags!" But Erin was laughing a bit too. "You're the old buzzard."

Venir shrugged.

"Erin, didn't you have any interest in learning your mother's craft?" Tatiana asked.

"I never had the patience for it. For most of my days, I've been surrounded by men and boys. I always preferred their company." Erin shifted in her saddle. "What can I say? I've been drawn to the action."

"No doubt you are fit for it." Tatiana quickly recalled that Erin was every bit the spirited butcher that her father was, and she had the same inner fire as Anya. "I think I'll enjoy meeting your mother. It will be nice to share with somebody from a similar background."

"I'm certain that she'll be happy to have your company. I think we bore her with our dangerous escapades. She worries about Venir, my brother, and me too much. And we aren't the only ones."

"You have a brother?"

"A half-brother, Brak."

"He's a warrior too?"

"More like a warrior and a half."

"What do you mean by that?"

Erin smirked. "You'll see."

Chongo's easy gait slowed to a stop. The pair of ears on top of one of his heads rose, and both tails stiffened, moving straight up in the air. The dog head with its ears still lowered growled.

"What is it, Father?" Erin asked as she rode alongside him.

Venir's eyes were fixed on a cloud of dust far ahead. A group of riders rode toward them at full speed. He reached down and grabbed his helmet that hung from the saddle. "Raiders," he said with a snarl.

WIZARD WATCH

"Gossamer, how do we kill this thing?" Grey Cloak shouted. He jumped away from the fiery stream of flames that one of the hydra heads spit at him. "It won't die!"

His statement had been true enough. He'd poked over a dozen holes in the hide of the monster, but it was still alive. It would quaver, only to heal by shaking its head then rebounding and attacking with renewed spirit.

Grey Cloak darted between the striking heads. He jabbed his weapon into the monster's scaly neck then ripped it out and watched the blood gush. The wound sealed as he sprang away from another attack. His own inner fire and the energy in his limbs were fading.

"I don't know that it can be killed!" Gossamer cried. The elven wizard stood behind a shield of magic while two hydra heads attacked. One head battered the shield like a ram while the other spit fire that splattered and sizzled all over the shield. The dome of energy began to splinter and crack. "My strength fades."

As Grey Cloak danced away from the monster's strikes, the energy in the Rod of Weapons began to fizzle. The spearhead sputtered, and he felt his own energy drain. "Nooo!"

For some reason, the failure fed his anger. The thought of losing made him mad. He would not succumb to a dumb beast. *I can beat this thing. I have to beat this thing.*

Grey Cloak did a high backflip over one of the monster's necks then landed on the balls of his feet. One head continued to spit fire while the other struck with its jaws open. He jumped high again.

The hydra heads collided in a collision of bone and fire then quickly went at each other's throats again.

If I can't kill them, maybe they can kill themselves.

"Grey Cloak, help!" Gossamer called. He'd shrunk into a crouch with his back against the wall and his trembling arms outstretched. The pair of hydra heads hammered him.

"No," Grey Cloak uttered angrily. "Nooo!" He charged the head with the Rod of Weapons lowered. New fire sputtered forth.

One of the hydra heads caught him coming from the corner of its eye. It struck him with a mighty force, sending Grey Cloak sliding across the stone floor.

He rolled back up to a knee only to be clubbed again by another of the monster's heads. His grip loosened on the Rod of Weapons, and it flew across the floor, out of reach. Three hydra heads curled before him. Saliva dripped from their fangs and oozed to the floor. He braced his back against the sealed door, panting and exhausted. "Horseshoes," he said.

The head in the middle sucked in the air, and its neck heated in a ribbon of glowing-hot scales. It turned loose a geyser of flame.

Grey Cloak covered up inside the Cloak of Legends. The roar of fire beat down on him like a crashing tide and knocked him into the wall. Cowering inside his suffocating shell, he was knocked around like a ball by the other heads. They beat, prodded, and nudged him, but he remained balled up in the garment like an armadillo inside its armor.

His body took a beating, but at the same time, he used the moment to think and gather his senses. His thoughts raced during the final moments before death. Cloak or no cloak, he could not survive the assault forever. Deep in the back of his mind, an old lesson he'd learned from Anya came to life. *The body can't move without the brain.*

Long before, when he trained to be a Sky Rider, he learned mostly about dragons but also about other creatures and monsters. Every living thing had a weakness. The hydra would have one too.

Grey Cloak grabbed the pommel of his sword. It was

one of the Sky Blades, similar to Anya's, that he'd chosen from the armory. He tightened his grip on the leather-wrapped handle. *Cut off its heads.* He flattened and played as dead as a possum.

The hydra's heads paused their relentless assault. Its cold noses nudged and sniffed him. One of the stiff heads rolled Grey Cloak onto his back.

He felt gooey saliva and fetid breath on his face. He focused, envisioned the creature hovering over him, and struck with the Sky Blade.

The sharp steel bit deep and sliced clean through the meaty neck of the hydra. The head rolled away like a ball of twine. Blood and gore dripped from its neck. An anguished roar blasted out of another head's widening jaws.

Grey Cloak came to his feet and propelled himself toward the next nearest head. It had not yet recovered from the shock and left its neck exposed. Turning his hips into the swing, Grey Cloak let the Sky Blade separate its head from its neck.

The remaining pair of heads was quick to attack. They spit at Grey Cloak with venom and fire, forcing him to keep his distance. He jumped from stone to stone, evading their attacks only to see them snaking away before he came too close with his deadly blade.

"Come on, cowards!" Grey Cloak baited them with his sword. "Fight like a dragon!"

The wary-eyed hydra snaked away again and again.

A bright-white light flashed, followed by a ring of energy that tied the hydra's necks together.

"Strike now! Strike now!" Gossamer urged Grey Cloak.

"You don't have to tell me twice." Grey Cloak closed the distance as quickly as a panther. He butchered the entwined heads and ended it. He walked away from the monster, using his gory blade like a cane, slid down the wall, and sat beside Gossamer. "I didn't think you were going to make it."

"Me neither. That's a first."

Together, they watched the hydra's body begin to melt and erode into a stinky pile of bubbling goo.

Grey Cloak's nose twitched. "Death stinks."

A loud, familiar roar rose from the bowels of the Wizard Watch.

Gossamer and Grey Cloak widened their eyes and exchanged a glance. Then the elves shook their heads, helped each other to stand, and said, "Bloody biscuits."

9

BISH

Venir buckled the leather chin strap on his helmet. "It looks like we have a score of raiders coming our way."

"We can try to outrun them. We aren't far from the city of Three," Erin suggested.

"No. Where there are twenty, there will be at least ten more lying in wait." He eased a large axe from an oversized satchel that hung from one side of Chongo's saddle. The war axe was a huge, menacing thing with razor-sharp twin blades that caught the sun. "I'll talk. If they don't listen, well, you know." He eyed Tatiana. "Fight or die."

"No problem. I'm getting used to it." Tatiana flicked her fingers. Wispy strands of mystic energy twirled around her fingers like snakes. "Is there anything you don't fight?"

"A good meal and grog, though it's won its fair share of

battles against me." He leaned over the saddle with his big axe resting on his lap. "Orcs. Men. All on horseback."

Erin lowered a metal skullcap with flared eyelets over her head then buckled the straps into place. Her large blond braid flowed down between her shoulders, and she drew her broadsword. "Don't forget we have Chongo," she said to Tatiana.

She nodded. "Yes, I've seen him in action. Back in Gapoli, when Grey Cloak and Dyphestive first joined Talon, Dalsay used the Figurine of Heroes and summoned Venir and Chongo. The lethal pair made quick work of the horde of goblins that they faced."

Even so, Tatiana's heart pounded inside her chest. She had little doubt that they would battle.

Her first fight on Bish had been an unexpected and nasty one. A small group of assassins led by a female sorcerer had caught them in the city streets of Bone. Before she knew what had hit her, she was flat on her back with the sorceress's fingers locked around her throat. Tatiana had dug her own fingers into the pudgy woman's soft neck, channeled the energy of Bish, summoned her wizard fire, and burnt the sorceress's head to a crisp.

That fight had earned her a pat on the back from Venir that day. They'd all treated her like one of them ever since.

The desert raiders rode up on them before they slowed to a stop, encircling them and outnumbering them more than five to one. They were a rugged lot, true to their name. The cloud of dust they'd brought with them passed.

Every man was covered in desert garb and a patchwork of armor. Some wore chest plates, and others wore chain mail that rattled. They carried swords, axes, and spears. Many of them were archers with arrows nocked on their strings. Ugly and scarred, they studied Venir and his group from head to toe.

A small balding orc in a black tunic atop a large chestnut steed spoke with a big voice. He carried a studded club in a strong grip that showed off his bare, muscular arm. "We'll take your gear and your horses. You can keep your freakish hound."

The raiders supported their leader with throaty howling and chuckles.

"Touch my gear or our horses, and I'll stick you like a pig, orc," Venir said.

"Brave words for a dead man." The orc introduced himself. "I am Kork, Prince of the Outlands." His yellow eyes narrowed. "You will do as I command."

"You are a prince of jackals and desert toads," Venir replied. He lifted his axe and rested it on his shoulder. "And if you don't ride away, I will kill every last one of you."

Kork swallowed. His men exchanged nervous glances. He caught their expressions and straightened his back. "Archers!"

Five raiders stretched their bowstrings and took aim at Venir.

"You listen to me, dog rider. I am a prince but not a merciless one. I only wanted your horses. Now, I will take your women. They will be my slaves and serve me at my beck and call!"

Venir flung his war axe as though it had been shot out of a ballista. The spike in the end gored Kork through the chest. His horse bucked and tossed him from the saddle.

The archers let loose their arrows, but not before Venir snatched up his round shield and charged Chongo into their ranks.

Thuk! Thuk! Arrows ricocheted off of Venir's helmet and shield. Others missed, while the last one buried itself deep in the meat of Venir's front shoulder. Using the hand on the same side, he ripped it out of his flesh and stuck it into a raider's neck.

Erin let out her own shrill scream as she spun her sword over her head in wide circles then attacked the closet raider, splitting the man's face from skull to chin.

Tatiana felt warm blood on her fist. Without thinking, she fired strands of energy like webbing from her fingertips and yanked three raiders out of their saddles.

A riderless Chongo trampled the men.

Venir was on the ground and pulled his war axe free of their leader. He plunged the blade deep into a desert raider's chest with a loud *thuk*.

"Tatiana, behind you!" Erin shouted.

Three raiders thundered into her path. One leapt from the saddle and tackled her to the ground. The other two tossed a weighted net over Erin, which tangled around both her and her horse.

Tatiana sent a shock of energy through the orc that piled on top of her. He leapt like a lizard, and Chongo ran him down.

Erin screamed, "Fight like men, cowards!"

The raiders dragged the woman on the ground across the rough and rocky land.

Tatiana summoned her fire. The bronze collar around her neck brightened with vibrant color and burned. *No, not now!*

The world began to fade. Her stomach started to twist and spin. She caught one last glimpse of her new friends fighting for their lives, and all at once, Bish was gone like the wind.

10

WIZARD WATCH

"TATIANA!" Dalsay called out.

She was on all fours with her hands and feet on the cold stone of the Time Mural's chamber. Her head swam, and her stomach twisted in knots. She retched, wiped her mouth, then spit. The hot atmosphere of Bish's sweltering climate was gone, replaced by cold. Goose bumps rose all over her.

Lord Catten and Lord Verbard floated toward her.

"Do you have it?" Lord Verbard asked.

Tatiana raised her weary head and glared at the underling. She glimpsed Dalsay's ghostly form standing nearby. She grabbed a leather pouch filled with sand from her waist and put it into Lord Verbard's clawed hand.

He inspected the contents and stuck his black fingernail

inside the pouch. With a nod toward his brother, he said, "This will do."

"Get started, brother. I will keep my eye on them." Lord Catten lifted his hand. Tatiana rose from the floor. "Tell me about your journey. Was it long? Was it short?"

During her time in Bish, she had learned more about the underlings than she cared to know. She wasn't about to give them what they wanted. She told the truth, but not everything. "Not long." She ran her finger between her neck and the collar. "I was stranded in the desert. I ran. I hid. I survived."

As she hovered with her toes one foot off of the floor, Lord Catten glided around her. "Interesting. Your clothing and tanned skin suggests otherwise... liar!" Tendrils like cords of lightning burst from his fingers and invaded her body.

Tatiana convulsed and let out a wild scream.

"No!" Dalsay called. "Leave her be! She did as you requested. Can't you see that she is exhausted?"

Lord Catten fired a string of energy right into Dalsay. The lightning passed through him, and his body shimmered and twitched with spasms. He felt excruciating pain. *Impossible. How can they do this? I am a ghost.*

"Did you feel that, you worthless apparition? Did you taste my sting?" Lord Catten's golden eyes glimmered like bright fires. "The power of the underling is matchless. Unrivaled. Your magic is nothing compared to mine."

Dalsay's body blinked in and out. He opted to stay down like a wounded animal. He caught Tatiana looking right at him. The anguish in her face was fuller than when she left. Her limbs were firm again, tanned, and thicker in sinew. She had been on a journey and had come back stronger than when she left.

Lord Catten grabbed her head in the palms of his furry hands and looked deep into her big eyes. "Tell me everything, elf, or I will boil your grey matter inside your skull. Tell me now."

"It's times like this that I really miss my brother," Grey Cloak admitted.

Another hydra head appeared inside the corridor. The monster crawled closer, revealing several more heads and long necks that swayed like snakes.

Grey Cloak counted out loud. "One, two, three, four... oh great, this one has five heads." He gathered the Rod of Weapons in one hand and said to Gossamer, "Would you rather use this or my sword?"

Gossamer stretched out his arm. "I'll take the rod. I pray I have enough energy to charge it."

Grey Cloak drew a dagger from his sword belt. "At least now, we know how to defeat it. I'm going for the head in the middle. That should even things out. Then you take your side, and I'll take mine."

"I prefer the plan where you take them all, but that will do." The arcane carvings in the black wood of the Rod of Weapons turned white. The head of the weapon blossomed into the shape of a sharp knife. "Good fortune to you, Grey Cloak."

"And to you as well." Grey Cloak rushed the hydra head in the middle. He sprang forward, landed on his feet, ducked, and rolled.

The other four heads struck at him at the same time. Their skulls banged into one another.

Grey Cloak popped up from the ground with his sword arm swinging. Steel bit hard into one of the hydra's necks. It thrashed with the weapon buried deep inside the meat of its neck. Grey Cloak jammed his dagger underneath its jaw. He yanked his sword free then chopped it through the neck again.

Four heads roared like one.

Slice! Gossamer decapitated the hydra head nearest him. Its flailing neck knocked the elven wizard off of his feet. Another head attacked the fallen elf. Fire shot out of the monster's mouth and consumed Gossamer in flames.

"Nooo!" Grey Cloak screamed. He jumped between two hydra necks, avoiding their jaws and dripping teeth. He swung his sword in the air then cut off the head with the fiery mouth. He rushed to Gossamer, whose flesh and robes were burning. He took off the Cloak of Legends, covered the man, and patted out the flames.

The hydra crawled closer. Three long necks sagged over the bulk of its body. The other heads swayed back and forth, eyeing Grey Cloak like a meal, their necks heated like hot coals. Fire ignited inside of their mouths. They unleashed their flames.

11

BISH

Lord Verbard sprinkled the sands of Bish on the stones in the pedestal. "Stop fooling with that creature, brother. Kill her and be done with it! Our triumphant moment is at hand as I add the final ingredient that we need."

The image in the Time Mural started to twist and shift. As if it had the view of an eagle soaring the skies, the picture changed. Great mountain ranges, majestic cities, and humble townships flashed before Dalsay's eyes. He saw the makeup of another world in an instant.

Tatiana screamed. "Guh!" Her voice became deep and rugged. "Get out of my head, dirty underling!"

Lord Catten blinked. His burning gaze dimmed.

Dalsay saw his opportunity. The fire in Tatiana ignited his own. He swept across the room and jumped into Lord Catten's body.

"How dare you!" Lord Catten shouted. He clutched his fist. "You will pay for this!"

Tatiana dropped to the floor, panting for breath. Tears ran down her cheeks, and her eyes felt as if they'd been boiled in water.

Dalsay's voice came out of Lord Catten's mouth. "Open the door, Tatiana!"

At first, she didn't understand, but the direction of Lord Catten's gaze showed the slab-door entrance to the chamber. She scrambled to her feet, tripped over her robes, then hurried up again. A long lever anchored to the floor pushed back and forth, using a fulcrum release. She jumped for it.

An unseen force scooped her off of the ground and sent her flying across the chamber. She slammed against the wall and crumpled to the floor. He bones ached, and sharp pain lanced through her shoulder.

"Foolish elf." Lord Verbard floated toward her with his black fingernails glowing red hot. "I have to waste precious time to kill you now." In his left hand he carried Gossamer's cane. He lifted it over his head and beat her with it. "Die, elf! Die!"

Dalsay's skull ached. He'd invaded the bodies of people before, but it was nothing compared to the evil metal trap that dwelled inside the underlings. The moment he entered, he felt alive again, but an overwhelming surge of evil crept inside him.

"Interesting," Dalsay heard Lord Catten say. The underling talked to him directly without words, but mind to mind. "Welcome to my world. A world you will not leave. Thank you for coming. Now, your knowledge will be mine."

"Nooo!" Dalsay called. Inky blackness snaked up his body and began to swallow him. He wasn't invading the underling's body—the underling had invaded him. It pulled him down into the depths of its spirit and slowly swallowed his soul. "Nooo!"

"Oh, yes. You will be mine, wizard. You will be mine forever," Lord Verbard said.

Dalsay clawed for freedom, for safety. He sought light through the darkness. As he was pulled into the bowels of evil, he heard a distant plea for help. "Tatiana!"

Through Lord Catten's eyes, he witnessed Lord Catten striking Tatiana with the silver handle of Gossamer's cane. His soul ignited. He reached down into Catten's spirit and found a pocket of mystic power. He wrapped it in his arms, made it his own, and unleashed it.

Lightning sprayed out of Lord Catten's fingertips and cut through Lord Verbard like a knife.

Verbard's coarse black hair stood on end. The fine hairs on his arms sizzled, and the gray skin started to smoke. He howled in pain.

"How dare you!" Lord Catten shouted. His fingertips continued to spit fire into his brother. "Get out of me, sage! Depart!"

Dalsay's ghostly body was thrust out of Lord Catten's flesh. He floated across the chamber, suspended a few inches about the ground, unable to move his limbs. He could barely think, and his head was splitting. He'd died once before, and it felt as if he'd died again. He cast his gaze toward Tatiana. She was on her hands and knees and barely moving.

I don't think either of us is going to get out of this alive. But we must survive.

Tatiana's eye swelled up. Her arms and back had lumps all over them. She'd done her best to fend off Lord Verbard's attacks, but Gossamer's silver-handled cane contained powers that blasted right through her.

Lord Verbard stirred. His robes and flesh were smoking. His silver eyes blinked slowly, and he shook his head. His eyes found the cane that lay on the floor at his feet. He stretched out his hand for it.

Tatiana reached down and jumped on top of the cane. She and Verbard wrestled on the floor, fighting for it. The underling was no bigger than she, but there was formidable strength in his wiry limbs. He clung like a vise to the cane.

"Elf, you will die today. I assure your death," Lord Verbard said.

Tatiana headbutted him in the jaw. "Stuff it!" She'd picked up a thing or two in Bish. Her new friends had a motto that stuck. "Fight or die," she said with a growl. Her hand slipped to her belt and found a dagger that Erin had given her. She rammed it into Lord Verbard's leg and pushed it deep.

He shrieked. With a wave of his hand, he sent her flying into one of the pewter thrones. The chair toppled over, and she rolled down the other side of the dais. When she fought her way to her feet, she held Gossamer's cane in hand.

Lord Verbard limped toward the pedestal of stones. "Brother, we must go. Kill them, and kill them now."

"Agreed." Lord Catten used one hand to fire energy into Dalsay and the other to attack Tatiana.

She caught Lord Catten's fire on Gossamer's cane. With an angry scream, she marched forward. Dalsay's ghostly form was being ripped apart. He spasmed. His face was a mask of pain. "Get out of my world!" she shouted as the power in the cane filled her.

With a flip of his hand, Lord Catten sent her crashing into the steps of the dais. "I don't think so, flea."

WITH BURNING bright spots in her eyes, Tatiana rose to her feet. Her nostrils flared, and she brought Gossamer's cane before her. She'd had, seen, and smelled enough of the underlings. They'd tormented her for more than a decade, and today, it would stop forevermore. Raising the cane over her shoulder like a sword, she let out a guttural scream and charged.

Lord Catten's face lit up with mild amusement. His lips twitched and curled. His golden eyes narrowed, and he turned loose his wrath. Strands of energy burst from his fingers.

Tatiana swung the cane like a club and caught the brunt of the fiery attack. The air sizzled, cracked, and popped. The cane absorbed the underling's awesome power. The black wood turned red hot. She marched on, inching closer and closer to the underling, taking everything he had.

Lord Catten hissed angrily and clenched his jaw. "You will meet your doom!" He fed more power into the cane. With a yank, he lifted Tatiana from her feet and pulled the cane free from her grip. He took the cane in hand and looked down on the woman lying at his feet. "Victory. It was inevitable."

The underling's robes dusted over her body. She shook from head to toe. Everything from her eyes to her elbow hurt, but she kept her eye on the prize, a bulge inside the pocket of Lord Catten's robes. She rolled onto her back in defeat, bent her leg back, and took aim. She booted Lord Catten in the groin.

"Ooooh!" he said with a moan.

Using every fiber of strength she had left in her, she rose and pounced. She and Lord Catten rolled across the floor.

Lord Catten's burning fingernails raked the flesh of her cheek. He pinned her beneath him and pushed the cane down on her throat. "It's been more than a millennium since I've killed with my bare hands. Feel my wrath!"

Tatiana ripped the Star of Light out of the folds of his robe. "No!" Her eyes flamed pink. "Feel mine!" She sent a shock wave through Lord Catten that rattled his bones.

He flipped head over toes, crashed into the pedestal, and fell at Lord Verbard's feet.

Lord Verbard wiped the black blood from his cracked lip. "Open the portal. Open the portal now!"

Inside the Time Mural, the world of Bish took permanent form. The hot sands were miles long.

With the pink Star of Light gemstone burning in the palm of her hand, Tatiana ran for the lever that would open the slab.

Lord Verbard shot more fire her way. It drilled her in the back and knocked her forward.

She reached the lever and pushed, but it was locked in place. "No!" An unseen force wrapped around it. Lord Verbard's telekinetic powers held it fast. "Nooo!" she screamed again. She put her legs into it and summoned power from the Star of Light.

The lever budged.

Tatiana's feet slid over the stone floor. She found a foothold and dug in. With fire in her eyes, she screamed, "Goodbye, underlings!" She broke through Verbard's hold and shoved the lever forward.

The stone slab slowly began to rise.

With his arms feeling like lead, Grey Cloak brought his long sword down in a two-handed chop.

The last hydra head fell to the ground. Its neck flapped

wildly, and blood sprayed all over. Its tremendous body quaked and heaved before it finally went still.

Grey Cloak stumbled backward and sat down on the body of the beast that a moment earlier had tried to kill him. His hands were numb, and every limb in his body ached. Sweat mixed with hydra blood and dripped from his chin.

"I hope you can handle another one," Gossamer said. He was slumped against the slab door with scorch marks all over him. His black-and-white hair was burnt to a crisp. He still wore the Cloak of Legends, and the room stank of burning hair and death. "As for me, I don't believe I can move a muscle. I'm spent of my energy."

Grey Cloak lowered his head. They'd fought not two hydras, but three, with the last one having six heads. "I don't know how we made it this far." He exhaled through his nose, waiting for the next roar of a monster being summoned. It never came. Instead, there was something else. He bent his ear.

Stone ground against stone, and the slab door started to move.

Grey Cloak raised his head.

Gossamer stood with his back against the slab.

Without thinking, Grey Cloak ran over to Gossamer and said, "The figurine! The figurine!" He rummaged through the cloak's pockets and snagged the figurine. He rolled under the door while the slab was still rising. He took a knee and lifted the figurine.

Tatiana and Dalsay were standing alone, side by side on the dais with the pedestal in the Time Mural chamber.

He cast a wary glance across the room. Images shifted inside the mural, moving on from one picture to another. "Where are they?"

Tatiana crossed the room. "They are gone."

Aside from the battle-weary look in the elven woman's eyes, there was something different about her. She was weathered and tough, not the polished sorceress she'd been before. She embraced Grey Cloak and squeezed him tightly. "I can't believe I'm this happy to see you, but I am."

Grey Cloak gingerly returned the hug. "That's good to know. What happened?"

Tatiana stepped back and led him in front of the Time Mural just as Gossamer wandered in. "It's good to see you well, Tatiana," he said.

She hugged Gossamer too. "You look awful."

"I'm certain I feel worse than I look." Gossamer faced the Time Mural. "They got away?"

Tatiana nodded sadly. "Not a moment after the slab began to lift. They dove into the mural."

"Where did they go?" Grey Cloak asked.

"Back home to Bish."

BISH

VENIR CAUGHT a resounding axe blow on his shield, grabbed a rider by the leg, and yanked the orc out of the saddle. He butchered the man who lay on his back in a prone position. *Chop!*

He heard Erin's desperate holler then turned to find Chongo's heads fighting over one man's body. "Chongo!" He pointed at his daughter. "Erin! Now!"

She was being dragged away in a net by two mounted riders.

Chongo sped after the attackers with sand spitting up under his paws as he ran.

Another raider bore down on Venir, swinging a curved sword.

Venir hacked the man out of the saddle. Every rider

that came at him fell under his wrath. His war axe, Brool, mangled their flesh, one by one.

He ran his spike through the chest of a beefy, one-eyed orc then picked up the raider from the ground, raised him high, and said, "This is what happens when you cross my path!" He slung the dead orc over his shoulder. "Who's next?"

There were no takers.

All that remained was the field of dead, who bled as desert stallions galloped away.

Chongo's jaws clamped down on the end of the net that Erin was entangled in. With his jaws locked and his leonine paws digging into the ground, he tugged back.

The raiders were jerked out of their saddles, and their horses reared then fell back on top of them.

Erin crawled out of the net with a scowl. She was scraped all over, and her helmet was cockeyed. "Thanks, Chongo."

Chongo sat and barked a loud "Raaah-uuulf!"

She straightened her helmet and realized she'd lost her sword somewhere in the sand. "Bone."

One of the raiders climbed his way back to his feet. He was a burly, fish-eyed half-orc wearing a leather breastplate. His big hairy arms flexed when he pulled a short sword with a hook on the tip.

Chongo growled.

"I'll handle this," Erin said. She marched toward her attacker with her chin up and her eyes locked on him.

The half-orc raider lunged at her.

She caught his sword arm by the wrist and pushed the blade aside. They fought over the weapon, pushing back and forth with the sword above their heads.

"You are a strong woman," the half-orc said. He kissed the air near her face. "I like it."

"Enjoy it while it lasts," Erin said in a cold voice. In a single fluid motion, she tossed the raider to the dirt and tore the sword from his fingers. Taking a knee, she pinned him to the dirt and slew him.

Another raider lay on the ground with a busted leg where a horse had fallen on him. His blue eyes were watery. He struggled to nock an arrow on his bow—it kept slipping from the string, but he finally got it. "Stay back! I'll fill you with this arrow!" he warned.

Erin walked slowly toward him. "I bet you miss."

"Heh! I never miss." The raider pulled back the string. "Goodbye, darlin'." He let loose.

Erin knocked the arrow aside with the back of her hand without slowing her march.

"Impossible!" the raider said with a wide-eyed, incredulous look. He dropped the bow, pulled a dagger with a blade of notched steel, and stabbed at her.

She sidestepped, kicked him in the belly, grabbed his hair, and kneed him in the face.

The dagger fell from the man's fingers, and she kicked it aside.

He looked up at her with a bloody lip. "Who are you? A warrior witch?"

She punched him in the throat. "'Warrior' will do."

"Erin!" Venir hollered. "Quit playing with that raider." He hauled himself up into Chongo's saddle. "We have a lot of riding to do, and I'm getting thirsty."

Erin retrieved her broadsword, sheathed it, and whistled for her horse. "Coming, Father." With her and Tatiana's horses in tow, she joined him.

"I see you lost your friend," he said as he began unbuckling the thin leather strap of his helmet.

"She vanished as if she was never really here at all."

"Bish happens."

A thunderous boom sounded out, as if the sky had been ripped open.

The horses reared and whinnied.

Chongo howled.

After the moment passed, Erin looked at the sky. "What was that? I felt the realm above and the realm below quake. Father?"

Venir's blue eyes burned like embers. A strange black

smokelike substance spilled out of the eyelets of his helmet. The blue veins rose in his glistening arms when he tightened his grip on his axe. His nostrils widened. His jaw set as his penetrating stare searched the area high and low.

The winds of the Outlands picked up. The tall cacti started to bend.

Dark clouds swept across the sky and quickly passed.

"Are you well?" she said to her father, who was sweating like a lathered horse.

"I haven't felt this in a long time."

"Felt what?"

"My helmet feels like a boiling pot on my head." His eyes shifted back and forth. "It has passed. But it was there."

She gave him a concerned look. "What do you mean?"

"When underlings were near, Helm would warn me. My skull would throb and pulse. My blood ran hot." He ground his teeth. "They can't be back, can they?"

"You're talking about the underlings, aren't you?"

"There is no other evil that made me feel like that."

"Tatiana mentioned two. Do you think it was them?"

Venir buckled his chin strap again then looked her in the eye. "I know it was."

"We need to return home, Father," she pleaded.

Venir turned his back and started to ride away.

"Father!" Erin dug her heels into the ribs of her horse, who sped after him. "Mother is going to kill you!" she said.

14

GREY CLOAK SLUMPED in an underling's pewter throne while Gossamer sat in the other. The battle with the hydras had pushed him past his limits, and he barely had enough energy to lift a finger. He gently toed a bottle of port that rolled down the short flight of steps to the throne. The sound of glass echoed loudly in the chamber. His belly rumbled. "Is there anything to eat in the tomb? I feel like I haven't eaten in weeks."

Gossamer, who was slouching in his throne, pushed himself up to sitting with a groan. "I'll fetch you something." He slid off the Cloak of Legends and handed it to Grey Cloak. "I thank you for this. It saved my life, more than once. It is truly a unique creation."

"My pleasure, but don't trouble yourself, Gossamer. Tell me where the food is, and I'll fetch it myself." The Figurine of Heroes sat on the arm of the throne. He tapped his index finger on the smooth head of the faceless figurine. He caught Tatiana looking at it from time to time while she and Dalsay worked behind the pedestal. He had no doubt that she wanted to take it. The hatred she had for it still lurked in her eyes. "Go ahead and say it, Tatiana. I know you are bursting at the seams to do so."

She raised her eyebrows. Like him, she looked like she'd been through war. Her robes and rugged clothing were covered in dirt and dust. Caked blood soiled them as well. The new attire gave her a warmer exterior, however, and he kind of liked it.

Tatiana approached the throne. "You know the harm it caused. You've seen it for yourself. Not only did it bring harm to this world, but it possibly caused great harm to another world as well."

Grey Cloak shrugged. "I agree." He shoved the figurine farther down on the throne's arm. "Take it. Please."

Tatiana's jaw dropped. She gave him a doubtful look. "You mean it?"

He nodded.

Tatiana came up the steps to the top of the dais, took the figurine in the palms of her hands, and eyed it carefully. "You've done a wise thing. I'm proud of you."

"Thanks." He wiggled his way up to a full sitting position then leaned toward her. "It's your problem now." He eyeballed her neck. "That's a nice piece of jewelry you are wearing. How about we make this a trade?"

"Huh?" She tore her stare from the figurine and touched the jeweled metal collar on her neck. "Oh, this. I'd forgotten about it." She turned her back to him. "With the underlings gone, I should be able to safely remove it. Do you mind?"

Grey Cloak undid the heavy clasp in the back and gently removed the collar. "There you go. What is this for?"

"The underlings created it. It allowed them to send me through the Time Mural and maintain contact so they could retrieve me."

Running his fingers over the beautiful jewels embedded in the bronze collar, he muttered, "I guess I can't keep it, then." It wasn't so long ago that all he ever wanted was a fortune of treasure, but the taste of gold and jewels had become all but meaningless to him. He offered it back to her. "Here. I have had my fill of traveling through time. I'd hate to imagine arriving in another world."

"Believe me when I say that Bish is the last place you ever want to be."

"Tatiana, come," Dalsay said in an urgent voice.

She hurried to the pedestal without taking the collar and joined him. "What is it?"

"I've been able to manipulate the stones." Dalsay half smiled. "It seems I have a stronger hold on my wizardry. I didn't think it possible. But it is." He pointed to the Time Mural. "Look."

"I see it," Tatiana said.

An image in the Time Mural appeared, similar to what they'd witnessed from the Eye of the Sky Riders back in Safe Haven's armory. It showed the surrounded area of the Wizard Watchtower. Ranks of foot soldiers encircled the tower, all of them Black Guard. Above the wild land, the Riskers flew. There were twelve middling dragons in all, led by one grand dragon and his rider.

Sitting on the edge of his throne, Grey Cloak studied the image. The surrounding woodland was thick, but in his gut, he felt that Dyphestive waited in the woods, hidden. "Can you find our friends?"

Tatiana set the Figurine of Heroes aside and passed her hands over the stones. "I can try. The Time Mural is simpler to manipulate in our own present time. Opening up passages to other places and times is where the challenge becomes vastly more complicated."

"We need to get word to Dyphestive and Anya and let them know that we have gotten control of the tower," Grey Cloak said. "From within, at least. I could go outside and warn them."

A pair of grand dragons dropped into view. They landed on the courtyard behind the Black Guards' ranks.

Grey Cloak stood. "It's Dirklen and Magnolia." His jaw

tightened. The mere sight of them made him angry. "We knew they would be dropping in at some point in time."

Dirklen and Magnolia climbed out of the saddles of their dragons. They were met by Black Guard commanders, who saluted them and kneeled. Dirklen ignored his men's efforts. He sneered and approached a sealed archway on the outside of the tower. He raised his chain mailed fist then pounded on the door.

The sound echoed inside the entire building.

"That's one loud knock," Grey Cloak said.

"What should we do? They are seeking audience with the underlings. If we don't allow them inside, they'll become suspicious."

Grey Cloak leaned back in his throne and locked his fingers together. With a smirk he said, "By all means, let them in. But let them wait awhile. I want to see them squirm."

15

DIRKLEN SCOWLED and balled his fists at his sides as he paced the courtyard. "How dare they. How dare they make us wait. When I get inside, I'm going to bust their skulls in," he said.

Magnolia leaned against the archway of the sealed door, her bright eyes as calm as the sky, and filed her nails with a metal file. "This isn't any different than any other time we've come. They take pleasure in your impatience. Don't let them get the upper hand on you."

Dirklen stood in front of his dragon, Waruum, holding the creature by the reins on its head. "I will feed them to my dragon. Let him feast on them. You can feed one to Molley." He rubbed his dragon's nose. "Would you like that, Waruum? You've never tasted underling before."

"I bet they taste nasty," Magnolia said. "I won't be feeding one of them to Molley anytime soon. No thanks."

"Ah, this is ridiculous. We have to report back to Black Frost. He won't be happy, knowing that Grey Cloak and Dyphestive are alive and we've failed to kill them." He tugged at the short hairs of his blond beard. "But if the underlings have gained control of the Time Mural, he might be happy."

"He'll never be happy. He's consumed by his hunger for more power. How long until he decides that he wants to feed on us?" Magnolia suggested.

"Don't say such a thing. That is treason."

"Almost treason."

"Treason is what Black Frost says it is, and I don't want to find out for sure." He pounded on the sealed archway again. "Let us in, you fools! By the order of Black Frost!"

"You aren't setting a very good example for the Black Guard. You sound like an angry child, and you are a grown man in his thirties," she said.

"Sister, shut up. I'll behave how I wish. Who is to question it but you?" He hit the sealed doorway again and again. "Open up, I say! Open up!"

Magnolia slid her fingernail file into a hidden sheath in one of her bracers then pushed off the archway. "You are only amusing them. Of that, I am certain." She swept her vibrant silvery-blond locks over her shoulder. "Why don't you step aside and let me give it a try?"

Dirklen looked at her like she was an idiot. "The door is huge. You have plenty of room. I'm not going anywhere."

She shrugged. "Fine." She raised a fist then politely knocked on the door.

The slab sealing the entrance started to rise.

Dirklen gave her a smug look, turned away, and marched inside.

Magnolia laughed and followed him.

From great heights in the sky, Streak watched the events on the grounds surrounding the Wizard Watch. Grey Cloak appeared to have safely entered the tower. Not long after that, in the middle of the morning, Dirklen and Magnolia landed. Shortly afterward, they entered. He circled a few more times before he made his decision.

I need to tell the others.

He peeled away from his position above the tower and made his way south to find them. He knew what to look for, and it wasn't long before he found them hiding in the woodland, only a fraction of a league away.

Slicer spotted him first. His middling brother waved at him with his wing. He pointed downward, and Streak joined the others, who were waiting below.

Dyphestive, Razor, and Gorva hid their faces with leather skull masks and sat in the saddles of the gourn.

Anya had a frown etched on her face, and Zora stood nearby with Waruum's dragon sister, Feather. Farther back, Cinder was hidden in the trees.

Cinder pushed his way through the branches then towered over the others. "What have you learned, son?"

Streak scanned the faces of the stoic crowd again. It appeared that no one was speaking with one another. With a shrug of his wings, he said, "I don't know what is going on inside the tower, but I know Grey Cloak is in there. Dirklen and Magnolia have entered as well."

"Is that all that you know?" Cinder asked.

"Hundreds of Black Guard soldiers have secured the grounds, but the elves that accompanied them have not returned. One grand dragon and his Risker are still accompanied by a dozen middlings." He scratched behind his earhole with his back paw like a dog would. "I really don't think that I have any good news to share. But I'm not sure that it is bad news, either."

Anya had both hands on her weapons' pommels. Her fingers tapped on the hilts. "I hate waiting."

"We need to let Grey Cloak know we are near," Dyphestive said as he turned his gourn north. "We'll ride into their camp and take a closer look at the matter."

"Do you think that is wise?" Zora asked. "You are walking into the jaws of death."

"I know," he responded, "but he would do the same thing for me. This is the plan. I'm going forward with it."

"It wouldn't be so bad if we could take off these stinking masks, but I'm game," Razor said. He wore Scar's bloodred hood. "Besides, it's been several hours since anyone has tried to kill us. I'm getting restless."

Gorva, who wore Shamrok's green mask, pulled her spear out of the ground. "Let's get this over with. I'm hungry."

16

"WAITING AGAIN!" Dirklen cursed. He and Magnolia were standing outside of the Time Mural chamber, waiting for the slab to rise. He faced the door. "I'm going to wrap my fingers around their scrawny throats and choke them to death."

"At this point, I have to agree with you, brother." Magnolia lifted her foot and examined the gooey substance on her boot. "They are vile things. What have they gotten themselves into?" She pinched her nose. "This place reeks."

"I don't know." Dirklen moved back toward the tunnel and ran his metal fingers around the rim of the exit. "There is a lot of this goo everywhere. There is no telling what strange activities they engage in when we're gone."

Magnolia said, "And I worry about the strange activities you imagine."

He wiped his hand on a hip. "And what is that supposed to mean?"

"It's only a jest."

"It didn't sound like one." He stared at the door again. "If they don't open it, we will. I don't trust these tricksters."

"That is a heavy stone. Do you think we can do it?"

"Not with our brawn. But with our wizardry, I have no doubt we can achieve it."

Stone ground on stone. The slab began to rise.

"There. Finally." He ducked underneath the slab and stormed inside.

Lord Catten and Lord Verbard were sitting on their thrones, drinking port.

"You have a lot of nerve, underlings! You better have a good reason for our delay!"

"Of course," Lord Catten said in a scratchy voice. "We have been very busy but have nothing but great tidings to share."

"Is that so?" Dirklen asked. "Then don't waste my time, underlings, and share."

Lord Catten gestured toward the Time Mural. "We have mastered our domain. The portal to our world is open to yours. We will be able to summon an army so great that Black Frost's forces will never be defeated." His voice cracked at the end, and he took a sip of port. "Please, see for yourself."

Dirklen gave both underlings a wary glance and said to Lord Verbard, "You are very quiet."

Lord Verbard only nodded.

"See for yourself," Lord Catten continued. "We've kept our word to Black Frost and delivered the promise. Can you feel that? You can feel the hot wind on your face and taste the dry sand on your tongue. Go and feel it."

Dirklen and Magnolia strolled toward the Time Mural together, eyeing the endless bright-blue sky and leagues of rugged land.

"It's a desert," Magnolia said with disappointment. "A wasteland. You call this a home?"

"You aren't seeing the bigger picture. We've bridged another world. Imagine what you can do with that," Lord Catten said.

The twins stood in front of the portal, each tilting a head over a shoulder. "What sort of creatures can we expect from this world? Giant scorpions and lizards? We have plenty of those," Dirklen said.

Magnolia chuckled. "They better hope that Black Frost isn't going to be as disappointed as we are."

"Don't worry, he will be." Grey Cloak appeared between the bonded brother and sister.

Their eyes grew to the size of saucers, and their perfect smiles dropped from their faces.

Dirklen sputtered.

Grey Cloak gave them both a hard shove in the back. "Welcome to your new home. They call it Bish!"

Magnolia's bloodcurdling scream of outrage would have cracked glass, but her voice was cut off when she went through the portal.

Lowering the Scarf of Shadows from his lips, Grey Cloak looked at Tatiana. "Did that really work?" he asked in amazement.

"I can't believe they didn't see through the illusion," Lord Catten said with Tatiana's voice. His body fell away in smoky dust, revealing Tatiana's excellent form. "It's hard to imitate an underling's voice."

"I thought the eyes would give it away. Yours were silver, and Gossamer's were gold. They were wrong, and I caught Magnolia giving you both a hard look," Grey Cloak said.

The body of Lord Verbard fell away from Gossamer, who stood with his cane in hand. "My illusion worked." A warm smile grew on his face. "I have to admit, that really felt good."

Dalsay dropped out of the ceiling and landed behind the pedestal. "Tatiana, we need to close the portal, quickly."

She ran to the pedestal then passed her hand over the stones, and the sands of Bish swirled up into her palm.

The Time Mural's image of Bish faded into a cold wall of stone.

Grey Cloak and Tatiana shared an uncertain glance.

Gripping her chest, she said, "My heart races! I can't

believe your plan worked, Grey Cloak!"

"I told you I'd think of something."

"Thinking of something is one thing. Having it work is another," she proclaimed. "I can't believe it." She rubbed her throat. "My voice cracked like dry wood."

Grey Cloak grinned like a fool. It had worked. His plan had worked. "As much as I can't stand Dirklen and Magnolia, I'm almost sad to see them duped so easily."

"They were overconfident," Dalsay said. "And sometimes fate will allow you a break. Today, we needed it."

Grey Cloak erupted in laughter. "Ah-hahahaha! Ah-hahahaha!" Tears streamed down his face, and he dropped to his knees, cackling.

"Are you well?" Tatiana asked with a tilt of her head. "Have you entered a state of delirium?"

"Perhaps." He wiped his eyes, and his chuckles started to wane. "No, no. I'm in good shape. I only wish I had a picture of the shocked looks on their faces. I wish Dyphestive could have been here. He'd have laughed his head off. We should celebrate. Gossamer, fetch a cauldron of wine!"

"A cauldron?" Gossamer asked.

"We'll have to postpone the celebration a little longer. We aren't out of the tower yet," Dalsay warned.

The Time Mural renewed the images of the tower's outside surroundings. Black Frost's forces were as thick as thieves, and Riskers still raced across the sky. "We still have to find a way to deal with all of them."

17

BISH

"Why did you let that happen?" Dirklen yelled at Magnolia. His hands and feet had sunk into the hot sand. He pulled them out and screamed, "You fool!"

"Me!" Magnolia flung sand in his face. "Don't point the finger at me! You are as much to blame as I am!" She shielded her eyes from the glare of the sun. "What is this place? It's sweltering."

Dirklen stood up. Sand ran down the cracks and into the crevices of his armor. "It's the underling world. Bish, I suppose." He pulled one gauntlet off and let the sand drain out of it. "I don't see a single tree. I don't see anything but rocks and sand."

"It sounds like the same view inside of your skull."

"Don't try to blame this on me."

"No? Why would I do that?" She patted at her sand-filled armor. "I'd hate to interrupt one of your tantrums. You lost focus, Dirklen. You let Grey Cloak get the jump on us, and now look at where we are. Stranded in another world."

Dirklen sneered and clenched his naked fist. "I swear, I will kill Grey Cloak when we return to our world."

"Ha. We don't even know where to begin. All we can do is make the best of our situation now." She slowly spun around and observed her surroundings. "Maybe this is the second chance."

"What do you mean?"

"Well, we don't have to worry about failing Black Frost anymore." She touched her cheek. "And I don't know about you, but my scar doesn't burn anymore."

Dirklen rubbed his scar. "It doesn't burn, does it?"

She shrugged her eyebrows. "You know me. I try to find the positive in things."

"By the looks of things, we'd better find water, or the only thing positive will be our inevitable end. And I'm not going to let Grey Cloak win. No, I will find him and break his neck."

Magnolia tousled the sand out of her hair. "Save your energy. If we do return to our world, I doubt it will be the same time or place where it started unless Black Frost gains full control of it, but our enemies control it now."

"I wouldn't be so sure." Dirklen started walking. "The Wizard Watch is surrounded by hundreds of soldiers.

There is no other way in or out. I seriously doubt that they will make it out alive."

She followed after him with her feet slipping on the rugged ground. "Let's hope."

"Forget hope. Look around. There is no hope here. The only thing we have is ourselves."

"Must you always be negative?"

"I don't see any reason why my temperament will change."

Magnolia nodded as she navigated the sparse terrain and said, "Agreed."

"We are home, brother. We are home!" Lord Verbard raised his hands to the twin moons in the sky and chittered with glee. "And we live again!"

Lord Catten's golden eyes twinkled like starlight. He took a deep breath. "Yes, we have cheated death through an unlikely course of circumstances." He wrung his hands. "But Bish is as ancient as we are. We could be displaced at any point in time, but I aimed for the nearest time to when we passed."

Verbard patted his brother's shoulder. "No doubt we will be close enough. No doubt we will have our vengeance." He studied the position of the moons in the sky. "Shall we journey back home to the Underland?"

"There is no place in Bish where I would rather be."

The underling brothers rose several feet from the ground and sailed above the land like a steady breeze. It was a long trek, league after league, day after day, and they were careful not to be spotted by the farmers in the fields they passed. They avoided small towns and cities, flew through ruins that appeared centuries old, and killed a caravan of halflings and humans along the way. It was an incident that never would have happened if a halfling had not seen them and snuck up on them along the way.

After long days of endless travel, their journey came to a halt at the base of the Underland mountains, which stretched north and south as far as the eye could see. Stark and massive, the towering snowcapped peaks seemed to reach for the clouds in the sky. It was an ominous and gloomy place made of rich black rock and little vegetation. Not even a single varmint nestled or crawled there.

Side by side, the brothers approached a cave entrance at the base of the mountain. The opening was half covered by thatches full of thorns.

"I don't like the looks of this," Catten said as he waved his arm. The thatches turned brittle, deteriorated, and peeled away.

They entered into a tunnel that began with a gentle downward slope before becoming a steep drop. It was darker than the bottom of an empty well, but they both saw clearly as day with their underling vision.

Deeper into the depths, they went long and far until Lord Verbard broke the silence. "Brother, where is the underlight? We should have seen it by now."

"I ask the same thing."

In the past, no man of any race or any beast dared travel into the Underland. The haven for underlings had kept them safe for millennia, for any who dared to enter never made it out again. Only death waited for hot-blooded men in the deep. The people of Bish avoided it like the plague.

The brothers' journey came to a stop on the edge of a tunnel overlooking a massive cavern large enough to swallow an entire city.

Catten placed a hand on the rock wall, and the under-light ignited. A soft blue glow spread along the rocky walls, through the stalagmites and stalactites above and below. An entire world filled with ancient illumination.

Verbard gasped. "How, brother? How can this be?"

The chamber that had once been filled with a thriving civilization of tens of thousands of underlings was buried under mountains of rubble. Rotten skeletons of underlings were scattered across the grounds in what had become a tomb of death.

The brothers angrily hissed. Vengeance burned in their eyes.

"We will get to the bottom of this," Catten said. "And whoever is behind the destruction of our people shall die!"

18

WIZARD WATCH

"THIS MIGHT BE the worst idea ever," Razor said to Gorva.

"Be silent and act like we belong," she replied under her breath.

In front, Dyphestive led the way into an army encampment of what must have been at least one thousand Black Guard soldiers. The outer ring of defense was comprised of troops of foot soldiers that carried spears. Behind them were the shock troops that fought with swords. The third ring of defense was made of a hundred soldiers in full suits of heavy armor that covered them from head to toe.

All of the Black Guards parted as Dyphestive rode his gourn through them like a great general in command of everything he beheld.

The stalwart Black Guard, each and every one hardened by fire and war, didn't dare a direct look at any of them. Such was the reputation of the Doom Riders.

Dyphestive rode his gourn through the spread-out rings of armored men, spaced thirty yards apart. The gourn breathed out smoke and took its time, walking at a slow pace.

At the front of the tower, two grand dragons guarded a sealed archway. They had the backs of their wings to the ranks and didn't so much as turn their horns to pay them any mind.

Skreee!

High above, dragons streaked through the sky and let out shrieking calls and hungry roars. The tension around the towers was thick enough to cut with a blade.

"What's he trying to do, count everyone head by head?" Razor asked.

"He's scouting," Gorva answered in her husky voice. "And letting Grey Cloak know we're here."

Razor eyed the tower. "Assuming he isn't dead."

"If he is dead, we'll soon be joining him." Gorva stared down a Black Guard who dared look at her. She pointed her spear his way. The soldier turned away and moved to one of his commanding officers. He whispered in his commander's ear.

"You really need to keep your voice down," she said to Razor.

"Why? They are too far away to hear us."

"Not everyone, it appears." Gorva turned her gourn in the direction of the Black Guard soldiers who were facing her and chatting. She lowered her spear and urged the gourn toward the men. The Black Guard commander swallowed hard, and the other soldier averted his eyes. As the others quickly cleared out of the way, Gorva pushed the spear to the commander's chest and locked her eyes on his.

The Black Guard commander snapped his heels together and saluted. The other soldier did the same.

With a firm thrust that didn't penetrate the commander's armor, Gorva knocked him down. She turned and joined Razor. "That should put an end to the questions."

"Well played. It looks like you have some edge to you after all. I like it."

"Don't get any ideas," she said.

"Too late."

Dyphestive led them around the tower three times then set his sights on another archway, its inside sealed with stones. It was on the opposite side of the grand dragons and behind the fully armed Black Guard. He passed through the ranks of soldiers as if they weren't even there, leaving the proud men gaping.

Razor and Gorva joined him in front of the archway. Not more than thirty yards separated them from the Black Guard, but they had plenty of space to breathe.

"Are we going to wait?" Razor asked as he fanned his hand under his skull hood.

"Stop fanning yourself, Princess," Gorva said.

"I've been inside before. We'll wait," Dyphestive said drily.

"I don't mean to pry, but what is really going on in that massive skull of yours?" Razor asked. "You've been spooky of late."

Dyphestive didn't reply. He sat in the saddle, still as a statue.

Razor couldn't even tell if he breathed.

"If he's not going to talk, then that only leaves you, Gorva. So does your mask smell as bad as mine does? I feel like I'm wearing an ogre's sock."

A loud roar scared the birds out of the trees in the surrounding woodland. It sounded as if it had come from close by. It was an awful sound, the howl of a wounded animal.

"Roooaaawwwhr! Roooaaawwwhr!"

"What is going on now?" Razor asked.

"That's the dragon's wail," Dyphestive said. "I've heard that call in Dark Mountain. The dragon cries when it has lost its master. Follow me."

They circled the tower then came to a stop. Dirklen and Magnolia's dragons sat on their haunches with their long necks outstretched, baying at the towers.

The deafening sound forced Razor to cover his ears. "Either they are dead, or those dragons really miss them. What do we do?"

"Stop covering your ears, for one thing!" Gorva shouted. "What are you trying to do, expose our cover?"

Everything she said would have been fine if she hadn't been shouting the last sentence when the dragons stopped their cries. Everyone, including the dragons, looked in their direction.

Razor said, "Well, at least it's not my big mouth that did us in this time."

19

"GORVA, I'll take the Black Guards on the right, and you can take the ones on the left." Razor snaked his swords out of their sheaths. "Dyphestive, I'll let you and your claymore handle the dragons. Sound fair?"

"Five hundred for me and five hundred for you. I can work with that," Gorva said.

The trio was caught flat-footed with nowhere to run. The Black Guards in full plate armor faced them with their weapons drawn. One of the grand dragons circled the tower and flanked them from the other side. Both dragons had their bright eyes set on them.

Dyphestive recognized the dragons, Waruum and Molley. He'd worked with them in the Dragon Den when he was a boy.

Waruum's black nostrils flared. The dark-scaled grand

dragon had gold eyes, each the size of a man's head. Golden tortoiseshell markings decorated the scales on his body, and he had horns like spears on his head. Molley was the same, but her eyes and markings were snow white.

In an ancient-sounding voice, Waruum said, "I know this one. The others, I know not." His hot breath came out like steam. "You are not the Doom Riders I know."

"No. We're cousins," Razor quipped.

"You are the ones our masters are looking for." Waruum brought his head down and came closer. "Tell us. Where are they?"

"Yes!" Molley said. "We don't sense them anymore. We don't smell their blood, either. Where are they?"

Their breath turned Dyphestive's armor hot, but he wasn't in the mood for talking. He grabbed the handle of his sword instead.

"I will melt you in your saddle," Waruum warned. "Tell me where Dirklen is."

Dyphestive scowled under his mask. "If your bond is broken, assume the worst." He lifted the iron sword. The red gemstone in the handle flashed in the sunlight. "And assume it's going to get worse."

"Destroy them, brother," Molley said. She sucked in a big gust of air. The scales on her chest heated up like orange coals.

Waruum's chest expanded as he did the same.

"I'm going to die like a burnt biscuit," Razor said to Gorva. "It's been nice knowing you. How about one last—"

Flames exploded out of the dragon's mouth, and the trio of heroes faded in the wroth heat.

Dyphestive's head swam. Between blinks, he went from outside to inside the Wizard Watch's inner chambers. He, Razor, and Gorva were surrounded by Grey Cloak, Tatiana, Gossamer, and Dalsay. The gourn were still underneath them.

Razor patted himself down, his eyes still closed. "Am I burning?"

"Open your eyes, you fool," Gorva said. She reached over and yanked his mask off. Her nose twitched. "I'm not sure which face I prefer."

Reginald the Razor cracked one eye open then let out an elated yelp. "Ah-ha!"

"Dyphestive, take off that hood, will you? You look like a giant scarecrow," Grey Cloak said in a voice full of cheer.

Dyphestive removed the mask and breathed easily. A heavy burden lifted from his shoulders, and he didn't understand why. He blinked his eyes to clear his head. He offered his brother a smile. "You live!"

"Did you ever doubt it?" Grey Cloak asked with a shrug. After his brother lowered himself out of the saddle, he hugged him. "Dirklen and Magnolia are gone."

"You killed them?" Dyphestive asked.

The group all stood inside the Time Mural.

"They've been left to a fate worse than death, I like to think," Tatiana said.

The Time Mural showed an image from outside the tower. The dragons, Waruum and Molley, still breathed fire into the walls. The Black Guard looked on in amazement as they backpedaled away from the wrath of the dragons.

Dalsay and Gossamer stood over the pedestal of stones operating the Time Mural. Neither one of them said a word.

"We are safe inside the tower. The walls are impenetrable. Every stone was forged with magic," Tatiana said.

"We need to get the others inside. Can we do that?" Dyphestive asked. "Zora and Anya are still out there, and so are the dragons."

Tatiana shook her head. "We can't hide in here forever. But we are safe for now. As for the others, we can't bring them in if they aren't close enough. But like the underlings, it will only leave all of us trapped inside. It won't take long for Black Frost to figure out we are in here."

"I thought we could move from Wizard Watch to Wizard Watch all over the world," Grey Cloak said.

"The underlings disabled that ability. They couldn't take the chance that you would use towers to expose them to the Figurine of Heroes," she said.

Dyphestive eyed the figurine in the palm of Tatiana's hand. "The figurine took them back?"

"I'm afraid not. They are cunning and opened a portal

to their world, into which they escaped. But they are not a threat to us now, nor will they ever be again," she said.

"Whoa! So you've defeated four big birds with one huge stone. That's what I call a sweet victory." He spotted a bottle of port sitting by the pewter thrones. "I think we need to take a little time to celebrate."

"We have to get word to Zora and Anya before we do anything," Grey Cloak said as he moved to his brother's side. "What is on your mind?"

"Can we go back in time?" Dyphestive asked. "The same as we went forward?"

"You want to save Leena, don't you?"

"No. I want to save them all."

Dalsay said, "We can't control where and when. We can barely control it at all."

A commotion started inside the Black Guard camp.

The image in the archway followed the direction in which the men were staring. Anya and Zora were being marched through their camp under heavy guard. The dragons were nowhere to be seen.

"What happened? How did they catch them?" Grey Cloak exclaimed.

Dyphestive pulled his hood on. "I don't know, but I'd better get down there and help them."

20

"WELL DONE. You've managed to get us captured. I hope you are proud of yourself," Anya said. Her wrists were wrapped together with leather cords, and a Black Guard shoved her in the back.

"Silence!" the soldier said.

Zora bit her tongue. She and Anya didn't get along, but the Sky Rider wasn't wrong that time. Not wanting to stay in company with Anya, she'd slipped away from the group that remained behind, opting to get a closer look at the Black Guard camp. She ran right into a Black Guard patrol of over twenty men. Without the Scarf of Shadow, she had nowhere to go.

Anya came, but because she didn't want to disclose the dragons, she surrendered.

The move surprised Zora—it was a sound decision. But

now they were being marched into the jaws of death, outnumbered five hundred to one, plus over a dozen dragons.

A loud shrieking filled the sky above. *Skreee!*

Flocks of drakes flew overhead, darkening the sky. The multitude of flying devils roosted on the top of the tower, while a few others scattered and clung to the sides.

"It looks like more of your friends are joining the party," Anya said to the soldier who'd shoved her. "Have you ever eaten drake before?"

"Gum up!" The soldier moved in and tried to shove Anya.

She deftly turned away and tripped him.

He fell face-first onto the ground then jumped up and wiped the grass from his face. "You'll pay for that!" He punched her in the stomach. "Ow!"

"What sort of fool punches a warrior in full armor?" Anya asked.

The soldier scowled at her. "When I'm done peeling you out of that metal suit, I'll teach you a lesson." He strutted over to Zora and punched her in the belly.

"Ulf!" Zora dropped to the ground, clutching her stomach.

"Mangy cur!" Anya shouted. "I'll cut you to ribbons."

"Anya, no!" Zora managed to say. She didn't want the situation to escalate any further. She forced herself up to one knee and slowly stood. Catching her breath, she said, "I'll live."

They were marched to a large tent that could hold many men in the center ring of the camp. The flag of Dark Mountain, its symbol a black mountain with lightning bolts crowning the top, waved at the tent peak. Two Black Guards carrying halberds stood by the poles that held up the entrance flap.

The Black Guard soldier who'd hassled the women stepped up to the entrance of the tent. "Commander Stuurg. We have captured two more spies in our camp. Do you want us to hang them?" He started to move back with his head tilted up then shimmied out of the way.

Commander Stuurg ducked underneath the tent flap and stepped into full view. He was bald on the top with a crown of coarse black hair circling the back of his head and hanging down to his brawny shoulders. His face was broad, flat-nosed, and clean-shaven. He stood every bit of seven feet tall and wore a black leather tunic with metal plates on the shoulders. His legs and arms were like mighty oaks, and his hands were the size of shovels.

"That is the biggest orc I've ever seen," Zora whispered to Anya.

"He looks like he might have some ogre in him," she replied.

Commander Stuurg approached with a hard look in his eyes. The points on his big ears twitched, and the skin between his eyebrows furrowed into tight, ugly wrinkles. He lifted Zora's face in his giant hand and looked into her eyes. When he finished, he did the same to Anya and clearly took a greater interest in her.

"A Sky Rider. I thought all of them were dead," he said in a gravelly voice.

"All but one," Anya replied.

Commander Stuurg backhanded her so hard that she spun halfway around. She staggered around to keep her feet.

"Silence, prisoner," he said with deep, slow speech.

Zora felt like her own breath had been knocked out of her. She'd never seen Anya hit so hard before. Her friend's lip was split and bleeding. To no one's surprise, Anya faced the orc again, staring at him hard, daring him to hit her again.

Commander Stuurg wiped his finger under his nose and sniffed. "I've never had the pleasure of breaking a Sky Rider before."

"And you won't be able to break this one," replied Anya.

He smoothed his greasy hair over an ear. "Torture is a matter that I take very seriously, but I won't start with you. I'll start with your vastly more fragile elven friend."

"Lay a hand on her, and I'll rip your poetic tongue out."

"You aren't in any position to make threats. You are surrounded by one thousand of the finest soldiers. Over a dozen Riskers are in our midst." He gestured at the tower.

"Look around. The drakes will be more than happy to eat you alive. So tell me, what are you doing lurking in the woodland? Are you with the men that posed as Doom Riders? And what are they doing inside that tower?"

Anya rose up on tiptoe and replied, "I don't know. I was hoping that you would tell me."

Commander Stuurg nodded. "I see. Ruprick! Fetch me my hammers. It appears that I'm going to have to do this the hard way." He touched Anya's cheek. "What a wonderful shame."

21

"Can't we use the portal and grab them?" Grey Cloak asked. The image in the archway had zoomed in on Zora and Anya, who had been captured by the Black Guard. They were facing a huge orc, who carried a short-handled war hammer in his grip. "I'm not going to stand here and watch them be tortured."

"Me neither." Dyphestive's jaw muscles and fingers clenched. "We have to help them."

"It's too dangerous. The Time Mural is not a simple doorway that you can enter and exit when you please. There are unforeseen consequences," Tatiana said from behind the pedestal. "You have to have faith in our friends. And it is possible that the enemy is trying to draw us out."

"I'm not going to stand here and watch my friends die!"

Dyphestive jumped into the archway, busting his face on a solid stone wall. "What!" he exclaimed as he backed away from the wall. He turned on Tatiana, his chest and shoulders heaving. "What have you done? Open up the portal. Now!"

Not hiding his displeasure, Grey Cloak said, "I agree! This is a dirty trick, Tatiana."

Dyphestive, Gorva, and Razor joined him, and they surrounded the three wizards huddled on the steps of the pedestal's dais.

"What sort of nefarious treachery is this?" Grey Cloak asked.

"Nefarious?" Tatiana almost laughed. "You saw the effort it took to get them in here. It won't be easy to grab more. We need a plan. We need to get them closer to the tower. We can't have you charging into the enemy's camp like a wild bull. This is bigger than them. Bigger than us. We are trapped inside this tower, and it's only a matter of time before Black Frost is alerted and he sends more forces. They will make it impossible to get out."

"Our friends might be dying." The veins bulged in Dyphestive's neck, and his voice cracked.

"They are more than capable. Let me remind you to have the faith in them that they would have in you. I do."

Grey Cloak had never cared for Tatiana's frosty demeanor before, but now, it was different. Before, her iciness was nothing more than a shield that protected her own insecurities. Now, there was no doubt that she could back up her strong stance with experience. There were calluses on her hands, and her smooth, tanned skin showed creases. Her arms and elbows were skinned, and she had dried blood on her clothing.

"If you have a plan, Tatiana, it had better be good, and it had better be quick," he said.

"It will be both. All of you, follow me."

Dyphestive looked between her and the portal. With a frown on his normally pleasant face, he shook his head.

Tatiana led them out of the Time Mural chamber and into the grand hallways of the Wizard Watch. Her ragged robes dragged over the granite floor as she spoke. "The Wizard Watch is ancient, and there is a reason why they have stood through time. They are well defended, both inside and outside."

"You make it sound like a fortress," Grey Cloak said.

"It sounds like that because it is."

They entered a large shaft that suddenly dropped to the lower levels.

Razor held his belly. "Oh, my stomach. It jumped into my boots. And I think I peed a little."

"Can you ever keep your comments to yourself?" Gorva asked.

Razor looked queasy. "No."

The shaft came to an abrupt halt. Outside was a short

corridor that led to a pair of ancient wooden double doors, rounded at the top and with large handles made of twisted iron.

"This is the Treasure House. This will be the first time anyone who is not a wizard has been inside here. We only open it in case of an emergency." Tatiana grabbed the handles with both hands and started to mutter an incantation.

Grey Cloak noticed Dyphestive's hard, impatient gaze on Tatiana. He was breathing down her neck, and his nostrils flared. It gave him an uneasy feeling he'd never experienced before. It was as if his brother had snapped.

The handles winked with light, and Tatiana pulled the doors open. Inside was a wall of shelves, and on those shelves were racks of potion vials, tubes of clear glass with cork tops and wax seals. Each seal was a different color, each color a variety of shades.

Razor stepped over the threshold. "This is it? This is the Treasure House? A room of fancy bottles?" He scratched his head. "Talk about a letdown."

Tatiana shoved the front of the shelving, and the racks of potions split in the middle, revealing an expansive vault within. Wooden treasure chests sat on the floor in neat rows. There were solid bars of gold and silver stacked along the walls, weapons racks filled with every melee weapon known to man, and several suits of armor.

"This is more what I had in mind," Razor said as he

wandered inside. He found a mannequin dressed in a suit of chain mail. A fine sword belt decorated the mannequin's hips. He slid out a dagger and flipped it over his hand. "A fine length of steel." He checked the sword in the scabbard and grinned. "It keeps getting better and better."

As everyone filed into the Treasure House, Grey Cloak said, "Wizards don't use these weapons."

"No, but our colleagues do. Even wizards need well-armed henchmen." She grabbed him by the wrist and pulled him back toward the potions. "This is what we came for. Their powers aren't lasting, but they will buy you the time you need." She started filling his inner pockets with vials.

"What are you doing? How do I know what these even do?"

She pressed a small pamphlet into his hand. "This guide will tell you." She grabbed several vials with gray tops. "Fetch whatever you can use. We need to return."

He eyed Dyphestive. "I know time is pressing."

Razor was stuffing a gold bar into his trousers. "Do you have a satchel I could borrow so I can haul more gold—I mean gear—out?"

Everyone grabbed what they needed then headed back to the shaft.

Razor hurried after them. The gold bar fell out of his pants with a clank. "Ah, forget it." He took one last look into the Treasure House then watched the doors begin to close. He picked up the gold bar. "I'm still taking this." He kissed it. "I need it."

22

COMMANDER STUURG BEAT his hammer into the meaty palm of his hand, making a notable smacking sound. "The strike against flesh is soft and sweet compared to the sound of bone cracking. I bet a warrior woman such as you would rather die than lose the use of her sword hand."

Anya was on her hands and knees and glared at him. "I'm not going to die, but you are."

"We'll see about that." He spun the hammer in his hand like a top. "Ruprick, get the spikes." He swung his heavy gaze to the Black Guard that had brought them in. "Have your men fetch a wooden bench, Sergeant."

"Yes, Commander." The sergeant saluted. "Right away."

Ruprick returned from inside the tent with a handful of metal spikes. His messy hair hung over his eyes, and he wore the uniform of the Black Guard, a burgundy tunic with a black mountain and thunderbolts on the chest over chain mail. He stood a foot shorter than Commander Stuurg and walked with a limp—one of his legs was shorter than the other. He offered the spikes to Commander Stuurg and said in a boyish voice, "Here you go, Father." The spikes slipped from his fingers. "Sorry. I'll get that."

Commander Stuurg closed his eyes, squeezed them tightly, and sighed. He opened them and watched as his son fumbled to pick up all of the spikes. He gently kicked his boy away. "Leave them alone, Ruprick. Go back inside."

"But I want to watch," Ruprick pleaded.

"Go inside!"

"I want to watch!"

Anya erupted in laughter.

Zora could barely stop herself from going into a fit of laughter. She trembled as she tried to clamp her mouth shut, but Anya's howling cackles were ripping her apart inside, and she finally let loose. "Bwahahahaha!"

The soldiers returned with a wooden bench and set it between the orcs and the women.

Anya stopped laughing, looked at the bench, and started laughing again.

Zora couldn't control her own amusement. She tried, but seeing Anya lose control like that tickled her. And it felt good to laugh. She hadn't remembered the last time she'd shared a good one.

Commander Stuurg's expression darkened. His thick

eyebrows like black caterpillars knitted together. "Silence... or I'll bust your skulls open," he warned.

Zora clammed up. Anya wouldn't stop laughing. Tears streamed down the older woman's cheeks. *She's losing it,* Zora thought.

Commander Stuurg brought the hammer down on the bench. *Whack!*

Anya quieted and blew a strand of her hair from an eye. She glanced at Ruprick then back at his father. "A chip off of the ol' anvil, I see." She started to giggle uncontrollably.

"Will you stop that, Anya?" Zora pleaded. It was impossible to miss the dangerous element growing in Commander Stuurg's eyes. Anya was humiliating him in front of all of his men and making a mockery of his son. The intent in his eyes was murder. "Anya, please stop!" she quietly urged again. "Please!" She focused on Commander Stuurg and opted to buy more time. "Commander, my comrade has not been the same since she took a blow to the head. She is not herself and means no disrespect."

"Yes, I do," Anya promptly said.

"I'm going to enjoy this. Black Guard, stretch forth her hands."

Anya's laughter ceased. She returned his stone-cold stare. "No need for that. I'll gladly give them to you."

One of the Black Guard put a blade by Zora's throat and pulled her head back by the hair.

"Any tricks, and I will end the elf's life." Commander Stuurg nodded at his men. They unbound Anya's hands.

Anya placed her palms on the bench. "Go ahead. Nail me to this plank of wood. I won't speak."

"Let me do it, Father!" Ruprick said.

She's lost her stones, Zora thought. *I have no idea what has gotten into her.* She started wiggling her hands free of the bonds that kept her arms behind her back. *If she has a plan, I wish I knew what it is.*

"Go ahead, boy. Show your father what a man you are and nail my hands to this wood. You can do it," Anya said.

Ruprick proudly spoke up. "I can do it. I'm a man now, Father. You said so."

"Quit calling me 'Father.' I'm your commander." He took a knee in front of Anya and clamped a hand over her wrist, pinning one arm to the wooden bench. "Move an inch, and your friend will die, Sky Rider."

"I thought you wanted information," said Anya.

"It's too late for that—far too late, thanks to your mocking tongue. Now, I want retribution." He looked at his son. "Pick up my hammer and grab a spike. It's time we taught her a lesson."

Ruprick picked up a hammer and spike then walked over to the bench. He might not have been as tall as his father, but he was still as stocky and well-built as most orcs. He held the hammer in a firm grip and placed the point of the spike on the top of her hand. "Here, Father—I mean, Commander?"

"That will do," Commander Stuurg said. "A few firm hits will do."

Anya tossed her head back and laughed.

Whack-ting!

23

Anya didn't bat a lash.

Ruprick hammered the spike again.

Whack-ting!

The surrounding Black Guard leaned in for a closer look.

Zora's teeth tingled.

Whack-ting!

"She doesn't scream, Father." Ruprick gave Commander Stuurg an astonished look. "I want her to scream!"

The Commander snatched the hammer out of Ruprick's mitt. "Silence, child. You should expect no less from a Sky Rider." He grabbed Anya's face. "You have a strong spirit. I'm impressed." He drew the hammer back and aimed at the defiant woman. "But your coffin will be sealed!"

Zora slipped free of her bonds in the wink of an eye. She activated the Ring of Mist in Commander Stuurg's face.

He coughed and sputtered while fanning his face and dropped the hammer on Ruprick's toe.

Ruprick hopped up and down. "Ow! Ow! Ow!"

Anya grabbed the bench and swung it around her body in a wide swath that knocked the Black Guard backward. She started pulling the spike out of the wood. Blood seeped over her grip, and she ripped the spike free.

"You are mad!" Zora said. She was holding her queasy stomach. "I think I'm going to be sick."

"Over the sight of a metal thorn? If that bothers you, you'd better not watch this." Anya pulled the metal spike out of the palm of her hand.

Zora fainted.

"Father! Father! Wake up, Father!" Ruprick whined.

Commander Stuurg began to stir. His son helped him sit up.

Anya scooped Zora up and slung her over a shoulder like a rug. Using her toe, she kicked one of the hammers into her palm. Surrounded by wide-eyed Black Guards, she said, "I see the fear in your eyes because you saw what I did. Get out of my way, or I'll unleash my worst on you!"

The sergeant commander took a step forward, sword in hand. "Don't let her out of your sight. Call for the spearmen. Sky Rider or not, there is nowhere she can go! There are a thousand of us and only one of her."

He was right. The soldiers surrounding her were ten deep. Fighting them alone was one matter, but while carrying Zora on her back, it was impossible.

Anya lowered her guard. "You are right, Sergeant Commander. I can't take down this entire army, but I *can* take down you." She pointed at him with her hammer and repeated the gesture to the others. "And you. And you. And you. Shall I keep going? So you need to ask yourselves, which of you is willing to die today?"

With his lips smacking like a fish out of water, the sergeant commander gathered the nerve to say, "We are the Black Guard. We fear nothing!"

"Good for you." She flung the hammer into his chest.

He dropped like a stone, clutching his chest and screaming. "Aaargh! Kill her, men!" He gasped. "Kill her!"

Anya sprinted through the gap where he'd fallen. Men collapsed on her from all directions. She sprang over them, leaping high like a deer. She jumped ten feet over their heads and raced for the tower.

They'd better let me in there, or I'm one dead Sky Rider. Plus one.

A fireball from the sky blasted the ground out from underneath her. She fell with only thirty yards to go to the tower wall. By the time she picked up Zora, she was walled off by soldiers in all directions.

In the sky, a Risker riding on a grand dragon soared by. A ball of energy charged in the palm of the rider's hand. He flung it at her.

She jumped straight in the air. The concussive force knocked her feet out from under her, and she hit the ground back first with Zora on top of her.

Zora stirred and woke nose to nose with Anya. "Awkward."

"An understatement." Anya stood. "Stay down. I'll handle this."

The grand dragons Waruum and Molley came around from the other side of the tower and positioned themselves in front of the tower's archway. "Don't let them get within a foot of this tower. Kill them first," Waruum said.

A war horn sounded.

Spearmen snaked their way forward through the rank and file and stopped no more than a few horse lengths away.

"Anya, before we die, I wanted to apologize for, well, going around you." Zora pulled a dagger and stood by her ally. "I hope you can forgive me."

"No. When this is over, I'm still going to get you. Don't die on me until I'm finished."

"Oh."

A Black Guard commander barked his orders. "Black Guard, advance!"

Grey Cloak, Dyphestive, Razor, Gorva, and three gourn appeared out of thin air and walked into the scene.

"No time to explain." Grey Cloak shoved a potion vial into Zora's hand. "Drink this quickly. Hurry!" He offered one to Anya too.

"I'm not drinking that," she said.

"It's an order," he said.

Anya snatched it out of his hand and sucked it down. Her lips twisted. "It's awful. What did you do, poison me? I want to die fighting."

The Rod of Weapons flared up inside his grip. "You're going to be fighting because now, you're invincible."

"I was invincible before I drank it." Anya nodded. A spring of confidence that she'd never experienced before flowed through her bloodstream. The corner of her mouth turned into a smile. "Not bad."

"The effects won't last forever. Only long enough to get us back to the wizard door."

"Spearmen, charge!" the Black Guard commander yelled.

A host of soldiers with long pointed spears bore down on the heroes.

Zora screamed.

24

ONE BY ONE, the spear shafts snapped against the heroes' bodies.

The big-eyed soldiers backed away.

Razor laughed.

Zora caught her breath.

Dyphestive pulled his skull mask over his head, madder than a berserker. He cocked the iron sword over his shoulder and charged into the nearest ranks. The first swing took two men down like one. The second swing split a man in half.

"That's not the plan!" Grey Cloak said. He parried and poked his way toward the tower. "Everyone, move as a group with me."

Razor and Gorva chopped down every soldier who came within the length of their weapons.

Anya yanked the swords strapped to Razor's back. "Mind if I borrow these?"

"Anything for you, Fiery Red!"

The well-armed Black Guard surged against the heroes, their commanders barking orders. "There is only a handful of them! Tighten the lines and chop them down!" The soldiers pushed forward, striking out with well-tempered steel.

It was a mistake. Anya weaved through their ranks as their attacks glanced off of her body. Her heavy armor and the potion of invincibility were more than a match for any of them. Her twin swords flicked out, separating soldiers from their limbs. She turned the battlefield into an onslaught.

Slash! Chop! Hack! She showed no mercy to the black army of men sworn to serve evil. She unleashed her own justice.

"Shield bearers! Forward!" one of the commanders called out in a panic. His ranks were being decimated by the assault of a lone woman and her comrades. The army was defenseless against their speed and steel. "Shields! Shields!" he shouted, looking horrified as Anya mowed a path right toward him.

A shield bearer handed the commander his buckler. He brought it to bear.

Krang! Anya's sword strike knocked the shield from the

commander's arm. She thrust her sword into his chest and ended him.

A soldier shouting a battle cry rammed a spear into her back. The tip broke off. By the time Anya turned around, a wild-eyed Dyphestive had chopped the man down. He swung the iron sword in huge arcing swipes that took soldiers down in twos and threes. He looked past Anya as if she wasn't there and kept moving.

Anya watched him go, looking offended. "He's killing them faster than me. I can't have that." Her arms started pumping steel into the enemy. She left a path of destruction in her wake. The dead piled up beneath her feet. The Black Guard ranks became disorganized, desperate, and sloppy.

"Tackle her!" a bold soldier suggested. "Tighten your belts and tackle the witch!"

"Witch!"

A group of soldiers formed a ring around her, and their leader said, "Now, we have her. Attack!" They all rushed forward as one angry knot.

Anya leapt high over their heads, backflipped, and landed behind them.

The soldiers collided. Armor smacked against armor, and men let out angry, painful screams.

"Aaargh! Get off of me!" one of them said.

Their battle-glazed eyes sought Anya. The moment they found her, she came down on them like rain.

Razor's speedy strikes dropped men like flies. Before one hit the ground, he killed another. The potion of invincibility gave him an edge he'd never had before. The enemies' strikes against his body felt like nothing more than rain drops. He took them out fast.

"Gorva, how many have you killed?" he called. He dropped to one knee, ducked under her thrusting spear, and pierced two soldiers with his twin swords. "I think that's twelve."

"I'm not keeping count," Gorva said. Using her spear, she gored a man then flung him over her sword. "But I'm sure it's more than you."

Razor cut two more men down. "Thirteen. Fourteen." He took a quick glance around. "Grey Cloak, I don't think your plan to get back to the tower is working. Our little herd has scattered. Dyphestive and Anya are bucking like wild bulls. I can't even see them."

"Stay with the plan!" Grey Cloak hollered. "We need to get to the wall!"

"'We' being the operative word. Only the three of us are staying with your plan." Razor did a head fake and shuffled his feet as a big-eyed soldier rushed him with a sword and attacked. He spun away with ease and cut the man down. "How long will this potion last?"

"I don't know!" Grey Cloak said. "Keep the ring moving toward the wall!"

"Will do!" Razor turned his blades loose and downed every man who crossed his path. "Sixteen. Seventeen. Eighteen." Not having to counterattack or parry made it easy. It fed his attack-first style and made him strong. He glanced at the tower. "We'll make it to the wall, but when we get there, how are we going to get through those dragons?"

Grey Cloak hollered back, "I'll think of something."

Gorva ran her spear through two men as if they were one. She headbutted another, rolled her eyes, and said, "Perfect."

The Rod of Weapons unleashed bright balls of fiery energy that blasted into the soldiers' ranks. Soldiers were knocked off of their feet, falling into one another and to the ground. They hollered curses and rose again to face the wrath of Grey Cloak. A bright light flashed before their eyes just before their lives ended.

We need to get inside the tower, or we'll be slaughtered.

Grey Cloak had the Cloak of Legends, but the others had little more than their armor. Zora, who fought at his back, had no defense at all. "Zora, listen to me." He slipped the Scarf of Shadows from his neck. "Take this and disappear."

"I want to fight!" she said. She had dropped almost as many as the others with her short swords. She downed a charging orc with a quick thrust. "It's not often I get a chance to fight like this."

"Take it!" he ordered. "We have to get into the tower, or this will be the last fight, period." He looked for Dyphestive and Anya. They were far away, like two swimmers who'd gone too far into the deep end of a lake. "Dyphestive! Anya!" he called. "Come back!"

25

A SEA OF RED. A wave of dead. Dyphestive let his anger loose on the murdering forces of the Black Guard. The evil powers of Dark Mountain, the servants of Black Frost... He wanted them dead. All of them.

Turning his shoulders into his swing, he blasted sharp steel through soldiers' bodies.

They jumped on his back, pounded on his head, stabbed into his neck and shoulders.

Dyphestive flung them off like children. He stomped a man under his foot.

A quick punch dented a shield bearer's shield.

Soldiers dove on his legs, tugging and pulling, trying to bring him down.

The iron sword went up then came down in an arc of death.

He showed no mercy. He faced a thousand-man army, and he wanted to kill them all.

The plan was falling apart. Doubt crept into Grey Cloak's bones. What was supposed to be a quick in-and-out mission had become a disaster. The dragons blocked the tower, and Riskers were landing on the ground. In the heat of battle, part of the group had become separated and were fighting with minds of their own.

"Guh!" Zora cried.

He turned and saw her clutching her side. Her eyes were as big as saucers, and she bled. He thrust the Rod of Weapons into her attacker and put him down.

"Use the scarf, Zora. Flee!" he ordered.

"I can't leave you. Not like this."

Shielding her from the attackers and fending off their attacks, he said, "Go back to the dragons. You need to escape. You need to hide."

Zora nodded. She lifted the black scarf over her nose and said, "Goodbye."

"Gorva! Razor! Tighten the ring!" he ordered.

They moved back-to-back, fending off the crowding forces.

"Have you thought of anything yet?" Gorva asked. "Because I'm starting to bleed."

The battle against the hydra had pushed Grey Cloak past his limits. It took all he had to use the Rod of Weapons. Its glowing blade of light began to flicker and sputter. He reached deep, channeled one more wave of energy, and shouted at the top of his lungs, "Aaauuggghh!"

A shockwave of power blew out of his staff and into the ring of the enemies.

Boom! The Black Guards were lifted off of their feet. Bodies banged into one another. Helmets were blown from their heads. Three rows deep of the enemy had fallen. They struggled to rise on trembling limbs.

"What was that?" Razor asked as he twisted his finger in his ear and wiggled his jaw.

Grey Cloak went numb from head to toe. He stumbled, swayed, and fell. Gorva caught him.

Anya and Dyphestive's warpaths crossed. With the two of them fighting side by side, the enemy fell at a quicker pace. The broken bodies of soldiers created a carpet beneath their feet. They marched into the slaughterhouse, led by screaming steel. Brave soldiers stood their ground and died.

Boom!

The alarming sound woke Anya from her battle haze like a slap in the face. She stole a glance behind her. Grey

Cloak had fallen. Razor's and Gorva's arms were up in surrender. *No!*

A dragon roared.

The soldiers scattered from the warrior's fury, leaving them in an open field with no one to attack.

Six Riskers on middling dragons landed and surrounded them.

Dyphestive let out a guttural howl like a wild animal. He lifted his sword over his back, lowered his shoulders, and started to charge.

Anya moved into his path and ripped the blood-soaked mask from his face. "Yield, Dyphestive!" She pushed back against his chest. "We are finished!"

His murderous gaze bored into his enemies. Veins bulged in his neck. "No! I will fight!"

"Listen to me! They've captured the others! If we attack, they will show no mercy!" She turned him around. "Look!"

Dyphestive's eyes started to clear. "I see them."

The Black Guard walled up around them, thickening between the Riskers. One of the Riskers, who wore an open-faced dragon helmet, called, "Interlopers! You are surrounded. Set aside your weapons and give yourself up to the supremacy of Dark Mountain."

Anya stuck her sword in the ground. Under her breath, she said, "We need to buy time. Do as they say."

Using both arms, Dyphestive stuck the iron sword in the ground. "I didn't think you were one for surrender."

"I didn't think you were, either, but here we are."

Tatiana stood in front of the Time Mural, her brow furrowed as she watched the entire outside scene develop. Their plan to rescue Anya and Zora had quickly descended into chaos. The dragons Waruum and Molley became privy to how to stop the heroes from entering the tower by keeping them as far away from it as possible. Now, everyone had been captured.

"We might not be able to draw them back into the tower, but we still have options," Dalsay offered. "This tower is more than a tower, after all."

"What was that?" she replied as she rubbed one elbow of her crossed arms.

Dalsay calmly walked to her, while Gossamer remained leaning against the pedestal with a weary look on his face. "The tower. Didn't the underlings make additional *modifications*?" He nodded at the pewter thrones. "Remember?"

Tatiana's back straightened. "They did. I'd forgotten how the tower was equipped. Has it ever been used before? Will it even work?"

Dalsay shrugged. "It has to work, doesn't it?"

"Gossamer, join me!" She hurried up the dais steps and sat in the chair on the right.

The disheveled Gossamer ambled over and took the

seat beside hers. "It's good to sit. I feel like I haven't rested in years."

"You haven't," she said.

Dalsay returned to the pedestal. "I'm going to link the thrones, and I'll be the eyes of the tower. It will be up to you to operate the defenses."

The Wizard Watch was more than a pillar of rock and stone. It was built to survive any attack or any siege. The only way to conquer it was from within.

Tatiana studied the arms on the thrones built by the underlings. When they'd made them, they'd linked them directly to the magic in the tower. Arcane symbols surrounded a dial, and buttons were engraved on the armrests. The buttons had many colors, and she didn't know the meaning of the symbols. But she did know what the tower was capable of and had been assisting the underlings when they built the thrones. So had Gossamer.

"Gossamer, do you understand any of these symbols?" she asked.

"A symbol is a symbol. I think I can interpret the meaning."

She nodded as her fingers caressed the pad of buttons. "I think so too."

"Who shall we target first?"

"You aim high. I'll aim low. We'll take it to the dragons."

26

 off the weariness and joined the defeated ranks of his friends. All of them, including Dyphestive and Anya, stood in the middle of the circle, surrounded by dragons and soldiers. Only Zora was still missing.

I hope she's safe.

With her bare hands raised over her head, Gorva said, "How is your plan coming along, Grey Cloak?"

"I'm working on it."

Razor chuckled. "My sarcasm is rubbing off on Gorva. I knew she'd come around."

The beefy Risker on the grand dragon patrolling the skies landed his beast. His dragon, an ugly beast with forest-green eyes and dark markings on his scales, lowered to the ground. The Risker stood in the saddle and removed his helmet, revealing a round bald head, sunken eyes with black rings around them, pale skin, and thin lips that looked more blue than red. "I am Craken. I am in charge here. You interlopers are my prisoners, and you shall be put to death by fire." In his own snobbish and highbrow manner, he added, "As I am a man of honor, I will allow each of you one last final word." He nodded at Razor. "Bring that one forward."

Two soldiers dragged Razor in front of Craken's dragon. They left him where he stood and quickly moved away from the dragon, who eyed Razor like he was a pork chop.

"Interloper. Share your last and final words. Make it quick," Craken said.

"Thank you, Craken. I'll be quick. I'm sure you don't want to miss your next meal." Razor ran his finger through his collar and cleared his throat. With a quick look over his shoulder, he winked at Gorva.

"Oh no," she said. "He's going to get us all killed before we even speak."

"First," Razor said loudly, "let it be remembered that I downed thirty-two of your men with my steel and my steel alone. Second, I think I deserve one last drink and a bite of grub. Like fighting, I hate dying on an empty stomach. And third, I was wondering, how did you get so many chins?"

Craken's flabby cheeks tightened. He stepped on his dragon's back. "Flame him."

Click!

A silence fell over the army.

"Hold!" Craken ordered. He turned his fat neck toward the tower behind him.

Click!

One row of stones in the middle of the tower started to rotate east. The row of stones below it began to rotate west.

The tower had the full attention of everyone, including the dragons.

An open portal replaced the stones in a staggered pattern. Dozens of metal pipes, about six feet long and with mouths as big as a man's neck, protruded. The rows on top aimed their metal pipes toward the sky, while the rows beneath aimed at the troops below.

Click! Click! Click! Click!

Craken narrowed his eyes. "What is that?"

A sharp whine coming from the tower pierced Grey Cloak's ears. On instinct, he crouched along with his comrades.

A ball of black fire blasted out of the pipe and careened toward Craken and his dragon then smote Craken in the chest.

Cha-thooom!

"Whoa!" Razor ran for cover.

Another blast erupted from the pipe and smacked into the hindquarters of Craken's dragon. He bucked like a mule and leapt into the sky, his wings beating.

The next thing Grey Cloak knew, every pipe began to fire.

Cha-thooom!

Cha-thooom!

Cha-thooom!

Cha-thooom!

Cha-thooom!

Cha-thooom!

Two middling dragons dropped from the skies and crashed into the soldier on the ground.

The Black Guard scattered like rats as their ranks were picked away by thunderous blasts that sent them flying in all directions.

Black fire and smoke filled the skies.

Men on the ground caught fire and were consumed by black flames.

Dragon wings burned. Their frightened roars shattered ear drums. They attacked the tower's turrets with their own destructive flames.

Razor retrieved his swords, pumped them in the air, and let out a triumphant scream. "Eeeyaah!" He attacked the nearest soldiers.

He wasn't alone. Taking advantage of the chaos, Dyphestive and Gorva burst into action. They grabbed whatever weapons they could find and cut down their enemies one by one.

Chunks of ground exploded all around them.

Cha-thooom!

Cha-thooom!

Cha-thooom!

Cha-thooom!

Cha-thooom!

The Black Guard fell by the dozens. Their commanders barked new orders.

Grey Cloak could barely walk. He tried to yell over the chaos. "Get to the tower! Get to the tower!" They needed to use the distraction to escape their captors once and for all and flee back inside the tower. "Dyphestive! Listen to me!"

No one listened. No one could hear him above the fray of battle.

Zooks. I can barely walk, let alone lift my arms.

The path to the tower had cleared. Waruum and Molley had taken to the skies with the other dragons.

From all appearances, the Wizard Watch had all of the enemy on the ground pinned down with nowhere to run. They rained terror in the skies as dragons were hit, wings blasted apart, and others soared away.

Cha-thooom!

Cha-thooom!

Cha-thooom!

The black pipes in the tower went silent. Inky-black smoke rolled out of the barrels. The battleground quieted. The dragons in the sky licked their chops and roared.

TATIANA PRESSED on the symbols of the armrest while Gossamer frantically did the same. "The tower's weapons have gone cold?" she asked.

"That's my summation of it," Gossamer added. Using his finger, he pressed one of the buttons repeatedly. "I thought the reserves were richer."

"They are deep," added Dalsay, who remained behind the pedestal of stones, "but the Time Mural draws upon the tower's powers as well. We are draining it. If we drain it all, we will be defenseless."

"No." Tatiana banged her fist on the armrest. "They'll be slaughtered if we don't help them. Dalsay, you have to get us more power."

"Give it time, Tatiana. The tower needs to draw from Gapoli's riches. If we deplete it all, the bond between the tower and Gapoli will be forever broken. We can't risk that. We'll lose our last hope if we do. I'm sorry."

She jumped out of her chair and headed to the Time Mural. The Riskers turned loose their assault of their weapons and dragon fire. Her friends were on the run as the enemy started to beat them down. She removed the Star of Light from the pocket in her robe. "We need to get word to them. They need to head for the archway. We have to save them."

"I'll open a door, but it will be dangerous."

The pink, gemlike Star of Light burned inside her hand. "I don't care. I'm going to join them." She hurried out of the chamber.

Gossamer caught up with her with his cane in hand. "I shall join you."

"You can't, Gossamer. You are exhausted."

"We are all exhausted," the soft-spoken elf said. "No one else is using that as an excuse, including you."

She clasped his hand. "Let's battle together then, shall we?"

"To the end," Gossamer replied.

They rode the shaft to the main floor of the tower then headed to one of the sealed archways. Tatiana stared at the door, tapping her foot, and looked up into the high ceiling from time to time. She understood what Dalsay was saying. The towers drew on the magic powers of the earth. They were needed to open the magic portals that allowed entrance. But things had changed, and they were going to have to open one of the doors manually—that had never been done before.

She let out an impatient sigh. "Dalsay, hurry up."

The door began to rise slowly, one foot at a time.

The clamor of the battle taking place outside carried into the grand halls of the tower.

Tatiana ducked underneath the rising door with Gossamer right behind her.

Soldiers, fire, and dragons were everywhere. Drakes darted down from their lofty heights and attacked. A drake set its eyes on the newcomers then dove right at them with its jaws wide.

Using the Star of Light, Tatiana's fist charged with power, and she blasted it out of the sky.

Gossamer leaned on his cane with two hands and said, "Well done. I believe you have their attention."

Scores of their enemies' eyes searched them out and came from high and low.

Tatiana nodded. "Fight or die, Gossamer. Fight or die."

Zora caught a bright flash out of the corner of her eye. A drake's wings were burning when it crashed into the ground. She followed its flight path and saw Tatiana standing outside a half-open archway entrance. Instinctively, she started to wave.

She can't see me. I'm invisible. But I need to tell the others.

The heroes were scattered all over the battleground. The ground burned in places, and oily black smoke drifted across the fields. She started picking her way through the carnage, trying to locate her friends.

Gorva rode on the back of a gourn. She thundered by Zora with her spear lowered, barreling down on a middling dragon and a Risker who'd landed on the ground.

Zora shouted, "Gorva, head to the tower!"

The orcen woman's eyes were set on the enemy. Her braid streamed behind her as she trampled soldiers in her path. The Risker's dragon shot out a mouthful of flames. Gorva and her gourn raced straight into it. Dragon and gourn collided in a crash of claws, fire, and flesh. Gorva leapt from the saddle, tackled the Risker, then vanished into the wreckage of dead bodies on the ground.

They are battle mad! I'll never get their attention.

It became impossible to locate everyone through the haze of the smoky battlefield. The air had filled with the roar of fire, cries of alarm, and shouts of pain.

Zora quickly wandered through the wreckage and spotted Grey Cloak, who squared off against three soldiers and battled for his life. His moves and attacks were quick as a cat's, but a sword-bearing Risker crept into his blind side with a sword in his grip, poised to attack.

"No!" Zora ran toward her friend, shouting, "Grey Cloak, watch out!"

Grey Cloak didn't turn. His parries fended off the enemy.

Running as fast as she could, she aimed for the Risker who had his eyes set on her friend. Her strides quickened as she hoped to blindside the Risker and knock him off his course.

The Risker stood only a few feet away from Grey Cloak. He pulled his sword back with two hands and readied the lethal thrust.

Zora lowered her shoulder. "Nooo!"

The Risker whipped his head around and turned, swinging his sword into her.

28

Zora's life flashed before her eyes. She saw glimpses of her childhood, her friend Tanlin, and the members of Talon, one and all, and she knew she would never see them again. The Risker's sword blade was about to take it all away from her with a perfectly timed swing. Her feet pumped into a backpedal. She slid across the battle-slick ground and started to fall. It wouldn't matter. Her move would be too late.

Thuk!

An arrow imbedded itself dead center in the Risker's skull. It stopped the man's swing. The sword fell from his fingertips, and he fell flat on his back.

Flaming fences! Zora stared at the arrow shaft deep in the man's skull. The black feathers on the end of the shaft pointed straight to the sky. Her heart jumped. *It can't be!*

She turned around on all fours. She couldn't believe her eyes. A spring of energy filled her. *Bowbreaker!*

In the midst of the chaos a few dozen yards away stood the tall, commanding presence of Bowbreaker. The stern-faced elven ranger's jet-black hair hung halfway down to his waist. His tanned, muscular arms went to work, pulling back the string on his long bow and letting arrows fly.

She waved, but Bowbreaker's focus was elsewhere. Every soldier he shot dropped dead as a fly.

"Not him again," Grey Cloak said.

Zora looked up at him. "Huh?"

Laboring for breath and drenched in sweat, he smiled and helped her to her feet. "I hate to admit it, but I might be half as happy to see him as you are. But where did he come from?"

A chorus of wild yells erupted out of the woodland. The air whistled with the sound of arrows firing out of the trees and piercing steel and flesh. Volleys of arrows rained death down on the Black Guard.

Riskers were knocked out of their saddles and fell through the sky.

"He brought friends," Grey Cloak said. "I didn't think he had any."

The tide of the ground battle began to turn, but the enemy dragons turned loose their fire, and the drakes darted from the sky and attacked the elven warriors darting out of the woods.

"Who are they?" Zora asked as she stared at the swarm of bare-chested elves. Their hair was long, and they wore only buckskin trousers. They fired arrows as they ran, swords strapped on their backs. There were hundreds of them.

"I don't know, but I guess all elves aren't bad."

"Tatiana!" she shouted.

"What about her?"

She pointed at the tower. "We need to get inside. She opened a door for us to enter!"

"It's time we rounded everyone up. Be careful, Zora, and stay away from the dragons."

Bowbreaker's arrival might have evened the odds, but they still had over a dozen dragons and scores of drakes to contend with. Grey Cloak needed to get everyone back inside the tower. He saw Razor hacking away at a group of drakes surrounding the warrior. He flung himself into the action and pierced a drake behind the wings.

"Welcome to the party!" Razor said. He sheared a drake's head off. "I hate to admit this, but my arms feel like lead. How about yours?"

"The same, but does your jaw ever tire?" Using his sword, he punched a drake in the chest.

"No," Razor replied. "Aren't these the ugliest chickens you ever saw?"

"Listen, you need to get in the tower. Tatiana has opened the door. Go!"

He chopped into another drake. "Can't they zap us in there?"

"I suppose not." Grey Cloak's shoulders were burning. He gave his sword strokes everything he had. "Now, go!"

Dyphestive faced off with a Risker who remained saddled on his middling dragon. He bared the iron sword before him. "Why don't you climb down out of your saddle and fight me, man to man?"

The Risker let out a haughty laugh. "Why, that would defeat the purpose of having a dragon. Wouldn't it?"

The dragon stretched its neck out and roared. Flames shot out of its mouth.

Dyphestive jumped to the side, but a toe caught on a body of the fallen. He tripped and fell. "Anvils!"

Flames consumed him head to toe and swallowed him whole. He lay in the midst of fire that should have burnt him to a crisp. The inevitable did not occur. His flesh didn't burn. His clothing didn't turn to ash. But the heat was real.

Energy pulsed through the palm of his hand. The red

gemstone built into the handle and guard of the iron sword glowed red hot.

Dyphestive rose in the flames that should have turned him into ash. He marched straight through the tide of fire and cut the dragon's head off.

"Impossible!" the Risker yelled. He scrambled out of the saddle, fell to the ground, and pulled his sword free. The shining dragon charm mounted into his chest plate cooled. Huffing for breath, he said, "You killed my dragon! I'll make you eat my steel for that!"

Steam rose from Dyphestive's limbs. "I love steel."

The Risker charged him at full speed with rage in his eyes.

Dyphestive stood his ground and put his hips into his swing.

Slice!

Steel clanged against steel. The Risker's head leapt off his shoulders, bounced off the ground, and rolled away.

Dyphestive raised his massive arms and let out a triumphant battle yell. He brought down his gaze, set his eyes on the enemy, and attacked.

29

"REMEMBER ME?" a gruff-voiced man asked.

Anya had downed more soldiers than she could count. She swung her gaze around and found herself facing the towering Commander Stuurg, who gripped a large war hammer. She brushed her sweat-drenched hair from her eyes. "How could I forget." She pulled back her slouching shoulders. "Let's get this over with."

Commander Stuurg's son, Ruprick, popped out from behind his father then squeezed the trigger on a heavy crossbow and shot Anya in the gut. "Who's laughing now, woman?"

Anya stumbled backward, clutching her belly with one hand. The bolt penetrated her armor and stuck out of her abdomen. "Cowards!" Her stormy eyes caught fire.

Thunder crackled overhead. Her sword began to shimmer. "I'll make you pay for that!"

A loud thunderclap was followed by a bolt of lightning fired down from the sky. It forked at the last instance and lanced Commander Stuurg's and Ruprick's bodies.

Their bones lit up inside their flesh. Every black hair on their bodies curled and started to smoke. Stinky flesh withered down to the bone, and they were left still standing but dead.

"Ugh!" Anya sagged to her knees. She pulled the bolt out of her belly and screamed. After she chucked it aside, she looked up and saw the massive face of the grand dragon Waruum and sighed.

"Time to die, Sky Rider," Waruum said, his breath reeking like a burning furnace. "Time to die."

Anya punched the horn on his nose and said with an exhausted look, "At least I'll die fighting. Do your best."

Waruum licked his chops. "It won't be my best. It will be my worst." He opened his maw. Strands of saliva connected his razor-sharp teeth from top to bottom. He coiled back his head and narrowed his eyes. "Goodbye—"

A huge shadow crossed overhead.

Waruum lifted his eyes to the heavens.

"*Roooaaarrr!*"

Cinder crashed straight into Waruum, and their humongous reptilian bodies wrestled across the landscape, crushing everything in their path beneath them. Their bodies locked together in a fierce battle of domination, raking their giant claws across each other's bodies and ripping scales open, biting into each other's flesh.

Anya came to her feet, stumbling as she fought to keep her footing. "Cinder, no!"

Waruum rolled on top of Cinder and pinned him down by the shoulders. "Today, you will die, old one!" He breathed fire into Cinder's face.

Cinder roared. His body twisted underneath Waruum. He curled his tail around one of Waruum's top horns and yanked his head back, breathing his own fire into the other dragon's face.

Waruum sprinted away like a whipped dog, spread his wings, and took to the sky.

Cinder coiled his legs underneath him and spread his wings. "Are you coming or not, Anya?"

She climbed into the saddle and grabbed the reins. "Ride the Sky!"

"You're badly wounded," Cinder said. One of his eyes had swollen shut, and there were burn marks all over him.

"So are you. Go!"

Cinder vaulted into the air, his wings beating fiercely against the wind as he chased Waruum. "He's strong and fast. Be careful."

Anya slipped a javelin out of one of the oversized quivers and charged it with wizard fire. Holding her bleeding gut, she said, "Don't worry. I have something special for him."

Grey Cloak stood caught between three Riskers riding middling dragons. The dragons' wings were spread, hemming him in in a circle of death. The Riskers pulled back their bowstrings then fired as the dragons spit flames.

Covering up inside his cloak, he jumped high. He was caught by a flying dragon's talon, which plucked him from the air.

Streak turned his head under his body as he flew away from the enemy. "Did you miss me?"

"Did I ever!" With desperate effort, Grey Cloak slung himself into the saddle. "Zooks! I don't have an ounce of strength left in me." Below, the Riskers' dragons spread their wings and launched into the sky. "It looks like my new friends are going to tag along."

"Sit down and relax. Let us handle this battle, dragon-style." Streak snuck behind an unsuspecting Risker who flew with her back to them. He locked his talons on her then lifted her out of the saddle.

She let out an angry shout.

"I'm sorry you didn't enjoy the flight." He dropped her. "Some people can't ever be pleased."

Grey Cloak smirked. He didn't have a lot of fight left in

him, but he grabbed a javelin anyway and tried to charge it with wizard fire. "I have nothing. I need to get stronger."

"What was that?" Streak asked.

"Nothing."

Arrows shot across the sky and zipped over Grey Cloak's head. Their four pursuers gave chase through the wind, firing volley after volley.

With the wind rippling his cloak, he said, "Streak, they are right on your tail."

"No problem. Hang on." Streak went into a barrel roll.

Grey Cloak's stomach flip-flopped inside his belly. "Please don't do that again."

Streak sped up, did a loop into the clouds, then dropped behind the four pursuers, whose heads were twisting around as they searched for the dragon. "How's that for flying?"

Grey Cloak groaned. "I prefer the straight line better." Flying wasn't as bad as he'd made it out to be with Anya, but his stomach still wasn't made of iron, either.

It didn't take long before the Riskers spotted them. They turned in their saddles and started firing their arrows.

Streak dropped below the first volley, rose above the next, and rolled left away from the third.

"What are you doing, Streak? You're flying right into the line of fire!"

"And they haven't hit me or you yet, have they? Don't worry. They can only fire one at a time, and there's only four of them." Streak shrugged his wings. "Besides, those arrows can't penetrate my scales."

The Riskers nocked new arrows with heads that burned like fire then took aim.

Grey Cloak asked, "Are you sure about that?"

"Hmm," Streak said. "That might be a problem."

30

Arrows whizzed by Streak's head like shooting stars.

Grey Cloak ducked. "That was close!" His fingers were locked to the saddle horn. His legs squeezed the saddle tightly, and his feet dug into the stirrups. "We need to break away."

"No. I have them on the run. Don't worry—we can handle this." An arrow clipped the edge of Streak's wing. "Barnacles! I'll make them pay for that!" He sped up.

"What are you doing now?"

"Vengeance is mine!" Streak caught up with the last Risker and bit the middling dragon's tail. It roared and bucked. The Risker bounced in the saddle, and his shot zipped into the sky.

"This is not a good plan, Streak! Let go of him!"

Streak's jaws held fast.

The Risker started to nock another arrow.

Grey Cloak rose up in the saddle just as the Risker took aim at his chest. The man pulled back the string and let the arrow fly. Grey Cloak caught the streaking missile with his bare hand. "Ah-ha!"

The Risker's white eyes bulged in their sockets. He started to load another arrow.

Grey Cloak ran along Streak's neck, planted his foot on the dragon's skull, and launched himself onto the back of the other dragon. He tackled the Risker, grabbed the bow, ripped it from the man's fingers, and flung it away.

The Risker punched him in the jaw while his other hand pulled a dagger free. He slashed at Grey Cloak.

"No, you don't!" Grey Cloak caught the man by the wrist and thrust the dagger backward. He caught a head-butt to the nose and slipped out of the saddle. The next thing he knew, he was hanging onto the saddle belt with one hand and several hundred feet of open air separating him from the ground.

Atop his dragon, the Risker leaned down with his dagger and started to slash at Grey Cloak's hands and fingers.

Pulling his free hand up to Streak's saddle belt, Grey Cloak moved out of harm's reach, below the belly of the dragon. "I need to try this again. Streak!" he yelled. "Quit fooling around and pick me up." He let go. The Cloak of

Legends billowed out, and he floated slowly toward the ground.

With a final yank, Streak released the dragon's tail, dove, and ran right under Grey Cloak, who landed back in the saddle. "Plan one didn't work out so well, but don't worry—I always have a backup plan." He let out a strange bark like a goose honking.

"What was that?" Grey Cloak asked as he watched the four Riskers turn their dragons around and move into a diamond-shaped attack formation. "Are you trying to let them know where we are?"

"Sort of." Streak flapped his wings and hovered in the sky, waiting right in their path.

Flames began to build in the dragon's mouth.

"Streak, they are going to run right through us. You need to move!"

"If you say so!" Streak's wings pounded the air. He shot straight above the enemies' attack formation.

The Riskers turned their dragons skyward in pursuit and ran straight into the path of Slicer and Feather, who came down like lightning in a storm. Their talons sank into the shoulders of the Riskers, and the dragons ripped them clean out of their stirrups. They flew off with them then dropped them onto the unsuspecting Black Guard below.

"Woo-hoo!" Grey Cloak shouted. "I didn't see that coming!"

"I had it planned all along."

"Good! Let's finish this!"

Tatiana and Gossamer teamed up and summoned all of the energy they had left. She used the Star of Light, he held his cane, and together, they created a force field that sealed the archway entrance.

No one came. Not one hero, not one friend, not one single ally. They were all on the battleground, fighting for their lives. So were Tatiana and Gossamer.

The first wave they fended off was a group of Black Guard soldiers that couldn't penetrate their defenses. The second wave was another matter entirely. The grand dragon Molley set her eyes on them and attacked.

Using her horns, Molley rammed the shield with jarring effect. She banged on the dome with her tail.

The shield buckled but didn't give. Tatiana felt every jolt in every bone of her limbs. She stood on one knee with Gossamer on both of his. Molley's tail went up then came down. *Wham! Wham!*

It took everything Tatiana had to keep her arms over her head. The Star of Light did most of the work on its own, but she had to control it. She was exhausted, her limits nearly spent. "Don't give up, Gossamer," she said.

"I won't. I'll die first."

Molley roared, prowling with her head low like a tiger

hunting its trapped prey. "It's only a matter of time, elves. But I hunger. I anger. I will make you pay!" The scales on her chest heated up like hot coals. She exhaled a fountain of flames.

Tatiana buckled under that broiling heat. Sweat dripped from her anguished face, and her damp clothing clung to her skin. The temperature inside the dome grew hotter and hotter. The Star of Light absorbed the energy, but it couldn't hold it all. The mystic gemstone started to smoke in the palm of her hand, and the skin on her fingers burned. She let out a scream. "Aaayieee!"

The shield began to crack. Veins spread across the dome. Fire became their sky.

"Hold up, Gossamer! Hold up!" Tatiana screamed. "We need to buy more time!"

"Time for what?" His voice cracked, and his cane burst into flames. "I don't have anything left, Tatiana. I'm sorry."

She hugged him and held the Star of Light up in her burning hand. "Don't be!"

31

Molley let out an ear-busting roar.

The dragon flames cooled.

The cracking shield held but flickered in and out.

Molley turned her back on Tatiana and Gossamer. Her tail, which had been hammering them moments earlier, had been hacked off, and only a stump remained.

Dyphestive stood on the battlefield, squared off with Molley. He held the iron sword in a high grip. The square ruby in the hilt burned bright as fire. He flexed his muscles, and his iron jaw was set. He charged Molley.

The dragon covered Dyphestive in a waterfall of fire.

He ran right through it and brought the sword down on Molley's nose horn. The blade sliced through the horn and bit into the bone of her jaw. She sideswiped him with her claws, knocking him across the grasses. He came to his feet and ran to attack.

Tatiana watched helplessly. She could barely lift a hand to peel the Star of Light from her fingers. The skin on her hand was charred to a crisp, and the entire hand burned like it was still on fire. "We need to help," she said with a moan.

Gossamer sagged on the ground. "I would, but I can't."

She rose on shaky legs then fell down again. With a dry voice, she yelled, "Kill her, Dyphestive! I believe in you!"

There weren't many people in the world who could beat a dragon one-on-one, let alone a grand dragon. But Dyphestive wasn't just anyone—he was a natural, and one with unusual strengths.

Molley set her wary glance on Dyphestive and kept her head low. Her jaws were slavering. "You are a big one. A juicy one. I'll enjoy my little feast when you are dead!" She lowered her horn and charged like a bull.

Dyphestive stood his ground.

Ten tons of dragon muscle barreled toward him.

"Move, Dyphestive! Move!" Tatiana screamed.

He brought down a well-timed swing.

Molley hit him first and flung him with her horns.

Dyphestive smacked against the tower about twenty feet off the ground, bounced, and plummeted to the dirt. His sword landed point first in the ground beside him.

Tatiana's jaw dropped. Her heart sank.

Molley turned to her. "Where were we, little elves? Oh yes, it's time to kill you. The question is, should I cook you first or eat you raw?"

"I prefer dragon soup!" Dyphestive shouted, yanking his sword free at the base of the tower.

Molley swung her head toward him. "You? Impossible!"

Thwack!

She reared up on her hind legs. An arrow with black feathers pierced her eye. A volley of arrows peppered her body like the sting of hornets. Molley let out a roar, jumped into the sky, and sped toward the clouds.

Tatiana waved at Bowbreaker, who stood in the distance, then dropped down on her good hand. "Whew."

Anya hurled javelin after javelin at Waruum until her arm finally gave out. She could feel Cinder's labored breath in the saddle beneath her. The dragons had been playing cat and mouse in the sky and spitting flames at one another. She knew her oldest friend was exhausted.

She gave him a shout of encouragement. "Keep fighting, Cinder. Keep fighting!"

"You know I won't stop," he said as he glided around in a slow circle, with Waruum doing the same a few dozen feet below him. "I will beat him."

Molley came flying up from the grounds of the Wizard

Watch on a straight path.

Anya stiffened. *Not another one.*

Molley had an arrow sticking out of her eye, and her tail was missing. She flew alongside Waruum. "We are routed."

Waruum took a moment to drop his gaze.

All who were in the sky took it in.

The Black Guard had fallen to the men and the wild elves. The Riskers and middling dragons had been defeated, one and all, and only little over a score of drakes remained.

Waruum glowered up at Cinder and said in his gravelly dragon voice, "Another time, Cinder. Another time." He and Molley turned their backs and raced toward the northern sky with a few handfuls of drakes and riderless middling dragons in tow.

Anya blinked several times. "Do my eyes deceive me? Or did they truly turn tail and run?"

"Well, one of them didn't have a tail," Cinder said with a chuckle. "But yes, they did. I wouldn't believe it if I hadn't seen it with my own eyes, but it happened." He gently bucked her. "We won. Ha ha! We won!"

The celebration on the battlefield was nothing short of an awesome event. Battle-weary men, elves, orcs, and even the dragons wore smiles bright enough to be seen a mile away. The battle was over. The battle was won. Against all odds, they were victorious.

Tatiana had her scorched hand wrapped in a towel dipped in healing salve.

Zora stitched up Anya's belly wound and kept having to tell her to be still. That conversation began only after Anya gave the half-elf woman a hug and said, "I'm not going to kill you."

Bowbreaker reunited with everyone, offering each a firm handshake, but he was the only one who didn't smile.

Grey Cloak patted the ranger on the back. "I know you can't smile, so I'll smile for you. But if you don't mind me asking, where did you come from?"

Bowbreaker said seriously, "I've been hiding from the elven monarch, Queen Esmeralda, for a very long time. She captured me once, but with *help,* I escaped. Over time, I built up new allegiances with the elves of the Wild and many others on the other side of the Great River. Our army is small but can move fast and hide well, and it's very effective." He put his strong hand on Grey Cloak's shoulder and gave him a knowing look. "I'm glad I could help."

"Me too," Grey Cloak said, noticing that one of Bowbreaker's arms was still more muscular than the other. "Were you behind the departure of the elven forces stationed here earlier?"

Bowbreaker squeezed his shoulder. "I didn't directly have a part in that."

Grey Cloak was about to ask another question when Dyphestive barged in and engulfed Bowbreaker in a bear hug.

"It's good to see you! I feared you had perished!" an elated Dyphestive said.

"Perish the thought," Bowbreaker said. He hugged Dyphestive so hard the young man's back cracked.

"Oh!" Dyphestive said. "I could use more of those. Let me do you!"

Bowbreaker slipped out of the way. "No thank you, big one. You certainly have grown. Where do you find the time to eat?"

"Hello, Bowbreaker." Zora opened her arms and gave him a hug. "It's wonderful to see you so well." She didn't let go.

Bowbreaker patted her on the head. "You as well, Zora."

"Some things never change," Grey Cloak muttered. He was happy to see his brother back to normal. He didn't know if Dyphestive had been kicked in the head again, but he no longer appeared to be brooding over Leena. He put his hand on his brother's back and led him away. "The fight isn't over, but at least now we can sit down and share a large meal. What do you say?"

Dyphestive grinned. "I'll start the fire."

32

THE NEXT DAY, all of the heroes had gathered inside the Time Mural chamber. The mural inside the archway was a blank slate of stone. Tatiana, Gossamer, and Dalsay stood over the pedestal of stones, talking quietly.

Grey Cloak sat in the pewter throne on the right, and Dyphestive sat by his side on the left. His legs were propped up on the arm of the chair, and he reclined comfortably on the crushed-red-velvet cushion, sipping from a goblet of port. "How are you doing?"

A half-eaten platter of food sat on a serving tray to Dyphestive's left. He gnawed on a turkey leg. He peeled the skin away with his teeth, chewed it, swallowed it, then said, "I haven't been able to stop eating since I started. I don't think I've ever enjoyed the process so much."

"I'm certain you have." Grey Cloak's eyes were fixed on

the Figurine of Heroes, which sat on the edge of the pedestal. "But eat up, brother. You deserve a feast for a monarch."

"We all do, after what we've been through," Dyphestive commented. He drank from a metal jug. "Ah!"

Grey Cloak scanned the faces of his friends. Zora spent much of her time talking to Bowbreaker. Razor and Gorva chatted amiably while sharing a jug. Streak lay in front of the archway as if it was the hearth of a fireplace, and all appeared well. But he couldn't stop seeing the faces of the people who should have been with them. Adanadel, the monarch knight, and Browning, the soldier. Grunt, the minotaur. Leena, Jakoby, and Crane were all lost, too, and he could never forget all of the Sky Riders who had perished in the wrath of Black Frost's fire at Hidemark of Gunder Island.

He remembered the Sky Riders who'd trained him as he sipped from his goblet. There was Anya's uncle, Justus, and the brazen father of Gorva, Hogrim. There was the dwarf, Hammerjaw, a lizardman named Fomander, and Grey Cloak's wise friend Yuri Gnomeknower. He recalled the beautiful elves Stayzie and Mayzie as well as their brother, Aric. Twelve Sky Rider apprentices, too, had perished. Not to mention his own mother, Zanna Paydark, and Dyphestive's father, Olgstern Stronghair.

All of them had died at the hands of Black Frost in one way or another. The heroes had scored a major victory the day before, but deep in his gut, he knew it was only one battle. The war would be much worse.

We barely survived this. And Black Frost's forces are ten times bigger than the army we faced.

He caught himself staring at the portal. Out of the corner of his eye, he noticed his brother staring at it as well.

"You're thinking what I'm thinking, aren't you?" Grey Cloak asked.

"Yup," Dyphestive admitted.

Tatiana approached, carrying the Figurine of Heroes in one hand. "And I know what both of you are thinking. But perish the thought. If you think we can use the portal to move you backward through space and time, you are sorely mistaken. It will take an immense amount of power and understanding to accomplish that feat. Farther forward and farther back will require even greater magic. Our only option is to move forward."

Grey Cloak swung his legs to the floor. "Are you suggesting that we abandon it?"

"Dalsay, Gossamer, and I have conferred, and we believe it best to destroy it."

Dyphestive leaned forward and knitted his brows. "You can't do that! We have to go back and save Leena!"

"I'm sorry, but that isn't possible. In fact, it's impossible," she said.

Dyphestive got up and stormed out of the chamber. A

few moments later, he shouted, "How do you get out of this place?"

"I'm sorry he feels that way," Tatiana said, still holding the figurine in her bandaged hand. "We believe it best to destroy the figurine too."

Grey Cloak slumped back in his chair, unable to hide his disbelief. "Are you mad? This might be the only way that we can defeat Black Frost, and you want to destroy it?"

"I'm sorry"—she started to turn away—"but the Wizard Watch has spoken."

33

DYPHESTIVE RAN INTO ANYA, who was splitting wood with a twin-bladed axe and tossing logs onto a bonfire. She was among the wild elves who remained busy, hauling away the dead and burying them in the forest. He stood beside her, staring into the flickering flames and breathing deeply through his nose.

She split a log of wood with a two-handed chop. "What has you in a lather?"

"Nothing."

Anya glanced at the tower. "Let me guess. Tatiana tweaked your temper."

He looked surprised. "How did you know?"

She planted the axe in a hunk of wood. "Because they are wizards. That is what they do. They deceive you. Why do you think I stay out here? I don't trust them."

Dyphestive picked up a large piece of oak and chucked it into the fire. "I don't trust them, either." Embers and burning ash drifted into the night sky.

"I was going to chop that piece next." Anya pulled the axe free. "Would you like to take a few swings?"

He took the axe in his hand. "Don't mind if I do." He began splitting logs one handed.

Anya tossed the severed pieces into the fire. "You fought very well yesterday."

"Thanks." He split another piece. "So did you."

"I know you miss your friends. I miss them, too, in my own way." She looked up at the starry heavens. "I really miss my family."

Dyphestive busted through another log.

"Tell me, what did you and Grey Cloak have in mind?"

"We wanted to use the Time Mural to go back in time and kill Black Frost." He stuck the axe in the wood then sat on a stump. "I know it sounds impossible, but I think it could work."

Anya tilted a log up and sat down beside him. They both stared at the flames. "And what did Tatiana say?" she asked.

"They are going to destroy the Time Mural. If they destroy it, we'll lose all hope of saving our friends."

"No offense, but they are dead. We can't bring them back. I know more than anyone how hard that is to live with." She reached over and rubbed his back. "I understand the guilt you carry because you weren't there. It's awful."

In the background, many of the wild elves were enjoying themselves by small campfires, singing songs and praises.

"They lost many today, yet they celebrate," she said. "Perhaps we should stop our mourning and celebrate the lives of our friends too."

Dyphestive shook his head. "I don't know if I can. There is a gnawing in my gut that won't go away."

"It will. Give it time."

He looked over at her. "Has yours?"

"No." She laughed. "And then again, perhaps that is the energy that fuels us."

He turned his head over his shoulder and beheld the tower. "Hopefully, Grey Cloak will think of something."

Once again, Grey Cloak and Tatiana were nose to nose in a full-blown argument.

"Explain to me how the Time Mural is a bad thing. It has caused us no harm," he said.

"No harm! Are you out of your skull? What about the underlings? They wiped out the entire Wizard Watch!"

He pointed a finger at her. "The Figurine of Heroes summoned them."

"And they sent you and the figurine through the Time Mural. Hence losing it and allowing them to stay for the next decade." She shook her fist in his face. "I was here, a prisoner, the entire time. I saw with my own eyes what they did."

Zora wedged herself between them and marched Grey Cloak back to the throne. "Both of you need to cool your skulls before they boil over and you say something you regret. We won a great battle. We should be celebrating." He pushed Grey Cloak back onto the throne as he tried to get back up. "We should be resting."

Grey Cloak grunted. "I don't want to argue with my friends. We have all been through trials. But the Wizard Watch is responsible for the Time Mural and the Figurine of Heroes. It is an error in judgement. We need to take this opportunity to correct our mistakes."

He lifted a finger and continued, "I want to say one more thing. How do we hope to defeat Black Frost with this small army? We are outnumbered one hundred, if not one thousand, to one. I have as much faith in my friends as any, but we need an edge. With the Time Mural, we have it."

"I agree," Razor said. "Let's go back in time and kill the monster."

Tatiana narrowed her eyes at him.

"Or not," he said.

"First," she replied, "we don't know that we can control time. We barely understand it ourselves. Second, we can't risk the Time Mural falling back into the wrong hands. If Black Frost were to control it, he would have access to other worlds, and he could destroy them. We must close this gate. And we must do it soon, before more of Black Frost's troops arrive."

"And what are we going to do in the meantime?" Gorva asked. "Run?"

"We'll hide, the same as we always have," Tatiana suggested.

"I've been dodging Black Frost's forces for years," Bowbreaker said with a nod. "All of you can stay with us."

"Thanks, but we already have a hiding spot," Grey Cloak said. Tatiana's words were eating a hole in his stomach. Everything she said made him mad. "We are all members of Talon, are we not? I say we put this matter to a vote."

"This is not a voting matter. We are the Wizard Watch. It is up to us," she said.

"What, the three of you?" He smirked. "What is the matter? Are you afraid that you are going to lose?"

"No, not at all. It's not about that."

"Good." He stood. "We'll take a vote."

34

"THIS IS FOOLISHNESS," Tatiana said. "Who is going to vote, and who will be discounted? Is Gossamer counted?"

"No. He's not a member of Talon, but you are. So is Dalsay, but his vote doesn't count because he is dead," Grey Cloak said. "If you'll excuse me, I need to fetch Dyphestive."

Tatiana followed him. "Why don't you let the dragons and the elves vote as well?"

He stopped at the chamber's exit. "You said it, and I agree."

"I'm telling you, Grey Cloak, this vote will not have any bearing on our current situation." She stormed after him, chasing him through the twisting corridors and criss-crossing to the main fountain level. "You need to let this go and trust me. You are asking the impossible, and it is too risky."

"We need to take risks if we are going to win."

"Listen to me." She grabbed his arm before he exited the open archway on the main level. "We might be a small force, but that doesn't mean we can't be effective. We need time to understand more about the source of Black Frost's power. Perhaps—"

"Perhaps!" He jerked his arm away. "We don't have time for 'perhaps.' We only have time for now!" He marched into the night. "If you'll excuse me, it's getting stuffy in there. Dyphestive!"

"Yes!" Dyphestive replied.

Grey Cloak joined his brother and Anya at the bonfire. "We are taking a vote on whether or not to destroy the Time Mural. I need you to come back inside."

Dyphestive looked over his brother's shoulders. "Why inside? It looks like everyone is here."

Zora, Bowbreaker, Razor, and Gorva were standing behind him when he turned. "What are you doing?" he asked.

"Following you," Zora said.

He moved between them and faced the tower. Tatiana stood inside the archway. She waved as the tower door closed.

Grey Cloak fell to his knees and screamed, "Nooo!"

Behind him, Anya erupted in gut-busting laughter.

"Oh, sorry, Grey," Zora said. "I guess we should have stayed inside."

The slab came all the way down and sealed the archway shut. He shook his head. "I can't believe I let that happen." He managed to stand even though he suddenly felt more exhausted than ever.

Anya put her strong hand on his shoulder and squeezed. "If you ask me, you are better off outside of that vile place. We'd all be better off if you never entered it in the first place."

He nodded his head. "You're right." He dropped his head and walked away. "Good night, everybody."

Grey Cloak found a private spot near the woodland, lay down in the grass, and looked into the sky. He usually rested very little, but it wasn't long before his eyelids became heavy and he fell into a deep sleep.

He awoke when he felt a hand touch his shoulder. He snaked out a dagger and put it against Gossamer's throat. "Are you mad, wizard?"

"Apologies," Gossamer said. "I didn't mean to disrupt your slumber. I know that you need your rest. But the matter is urgent."

Grey Cloak rolled onto his side. "If it's urgent, why don't you tell Tatiana?"

"No, I wouldn't do that. It's about the Time Mural. Let's say that... well, I don't agree with her."

Grey Cloak sat up and looked Gossamer in the eye. "You don't?"

"Not at all. I feel that the only way to stop Black Frost is by going back. Your plan is best."

He put his dagger away. "I didn't think going back was possible."

"It can be done, but not without a degree of risk. Tatiana won't take that risk, but I believe we have to. Do you want to try?" Gossamer asked.

"What about the others?"

"They can't all go. I'm only set up to steal one more into the tower. And time is pressing. We need to do this now, while Tatiana and Dalsay are distracted."

Grey Cloak planted a foot and stood. "Distracted with what?"

"They are working on opening the doorways to the other towers. If you are coming along, you need to come along now."

"I need to get Dyphestive."

"Hurry, and be discreet about it. Go to the archway entrance." Gossamer's body started to fade, and with a few twinkles of light, he vanished.

Grey Cloak picked up the Rod of Weapons and stole his way into camp, where plenty of wild elves leaned over their campfires. They didn't pay him any mind. He found Dyphestive talking to Anya at the Bonfire.

What is going on with the two of them? Grey Cloak interrupted. "Excuse me, but can I borrow my brother for a moment?"

Anya shrugged and flipped a strip of bark into the fire.

Dyphestive slapped his hands on his knees then rose. "I'll return shortly."

"Yes, we'll only be a moment." Grey Cloak pulled his brother toward the tower. Once he was out of earshot of Anya, he said, "We are going through the Time Mural."

"What do you mean? How?" He craned his neck toward the camp. "What about the others?"

"Keep your voice down and don't act suspicious. It's only us."

"We can't leave without telling them."

"Do you want to come or not? I'll leave without you, if I must." He headed to the archway. "Will you come, brother?"

"I need my sword."

"There isn't time for that. We must make haste, and it will alert the others." His body began to fade. "Are you coming? Hurry!"

Anya looked over a shoulder and caught Dyphestive's eye. She rose and marched their way.

"Come now!" Grey Cloak urged.

Anya came running.

Dyphestive backpedaled and waved at her.

Both brothers disappeared.

The last thing Grey Cloak heard was Anya's curse.

35

"ANYA, WHAT HAPPENED?" Zora asked. She was sound asleep when she'd awakened to hear the Sky Rider shouting. The warrior woman was in full battle mode, eyes blazing as she chopped into the tower's entrance. "Stop, Anya!"

The Sky Rider's heated gaze bored into Zora like a hot knife cutting through butter. "They took them!"

Zora yawned and rubbed her eyes. "They took who?"

"Grey Cloak and Dyphestive."

Razor strolled up and asked, "What's going on, ladies? Were you starting another celebration without me?" He scratched his bare chest, wearing only his trousers. He buckled on his sword belt. "I always feel naked without my gear."

Zora rolled her eyes. "Will you put on a jerkin?"

"I would, but one of the wild elven women took it, er...

to wash it." He rocked back and forth on his heels and studied the tower. "Eh, what is going on?"

"Grey Cloak and Dyphestive disappeared into the tower," Anya stated. "I warned everyone that no good comes from the Wizard Watch."

"They are hardly the enemy," Zora added. "Maybe Tatiana wanted to talk to them again."

Anya shook her head. "No. Grey Cloak hustled Dyphestive off only a few minutes ago for some reason. He came by the fire and appeared to be in a hurry. I didn't think anything of it until I saw them disappear. I think he was trying to warn Dyphestive about something, and the wizards took him."

"That doesn't make any sense. Why would Tatiana take Grey Cloak? They don't get along," Zora said. She cupped her hands around her mouth and shouted up at the tower, "Tatiana! Tatiana!"

"What do you think you are doing? I've been doing that," said Anya.

"Yes, but she doesn't like you."

"She likes me," Razor said with a smile. "After all, I was her retainer back when all of us met. She'll listen to me. Tatiana! It's your favorite swordsman! Open up so we can talk."

Gorva hurried over with her spear in hand. "Why are you yelling at the tower? You look like a bunch of fools."

"Tatiana stole Grey Cloak and Dyphestive," Anya said.

"No, she didn't," Zora said. "She wouldn't steal them." She sighed. "We need to wait this out. And Gorva is right—we do look like fools yelling at a tower. I'm going back to the bonfire to wait."

Razor stretched his arms overhead and yawned. "I agree. I'll be inside my tent. If anyone shows up, wake me. But knock first, in case I have company." He winked at Anya. "That's the courteous thing to do."

Zora and Razor departed, leaving Anya and Gorva alone at the base of the tower.

"You really hate the wizards, don't you?" Gorva asked.

"My family never trusted them. The Sky Riders had difficulty working with them. They always have their own agenda."

"I know my father distrusted them too," Gorva said.

"We haven't spoken much, but I knew your father well. He was a great Sky Rider."

"Yes, and if he were here, he'd be helping you try to bust open that tower."

"Quickly. Quickly," Gossamer said.

Grey Cloak and Dyphestive arrived in the main fountain chamber on the other side of the archway wall. Gossamer met them there and hurried them back toward the Time Mural chamber.

"We have to avoid our friends. They won't understand, but I am with you. The only way to stop Black Frost is to destroy him in the past." Gossamer rushed up a flight of moving stairs that switched back and forth on the way to the top. They arrived outside of the Time Mural chamber and hastened inside. "Pull the lever. Pull the lever."

Dyphestive did as he was told, and the slab door closed.

The Time Mural was no longer a solid stone wall but rather a huge picture of changing views of Gapoli's landscape. There were glimpses of small towns, sprawling farmland, the sloping hills of the plains, and deep valleys of woodland. The images changed in a wink.

"Streak!" Grey Cloak rushed to his dragon, who was lying where Grey Cloak had left him. "Streak?"

Gossamer moved behind the pedestal. "He has not budged an inch. We tried to wake him, but he will not move."

Grey Cloak knocked on his dragon's head with the rod. "Will you wake up?"

The middling dragon didn't lift a lash.

Grey Cloak tilted his head. "That's strange."

"Take your positions in front of the mural. Hurry," Gossamer urged them.

Dyphestive joined Grey Cloak and faced an archway big enough for a grand dragon to fit through. "Where are you going to send us?"

Gossamer's hands were busy organizing the precious

stones. A multitude of colors shone on his face like a scintillating sunbeam. "I'm going to send you as far back in the past as I can. Several years, I hope. I hope I can send you back further than the Day of Betrayal. You can warn the others about Black Frost."

Dyphestive glanced down at his brother. "That's a long way back. Are you certain about this?"

Grey Cloak stared into the mural and smirked. "I'll take my chances."

Dyphestive bobbed his chin. "Me too."

The lever that closed the archway flipped over. Dalsay appeared by the handle. The slab started to rise. "Gossamer, what are you doing?"

"What you should have done," Gossamer said.

Tatiana's legs appeared behind the rising slab.

Gossamer had an intense look. "Go now! I can't hold the image any longer!"

Grey Cloak and Dyphestive jumped into the portal.

Tatiana ran into the chamber. The archway was nothing more than a stone wall. She fastened her eyes on Gossamer. "Gossamer! Why did you do this? Explain yourself!"

"I'm sorry, dear friend. I only did what I was ordered to

do. Long live Black Frost." Gossamer twisted a silver ring on his finger then disappeared in a flash of light. The pedestal exploded.

36

Zora paced around the bonfire. It had been hours since Grey Cloak and Dyphestive had disappeared, and the early-morning sun had risen. The rich song of the birds was with her, and her belly growled.

"You need to eat. They might not come out for days," Anya said. She'd been sitting on a wood stump all night long, using a dagger to carve straight branches into spears. "And we can't wait out here forever. There is no telling what is going on in there."

"We can't leave without our leader," she said.

"No, but we can't wait for more of Black Frost's forces to arrive, either. Face it—we aren't much better off than we were before. We are back where we started."

"What makes you say such a thing?"

Anya shrugged. "My gut instinct tells me."

"Your gut instinct is horrible."

"Perhaps, but you'll never see me disappear inside one of those towers." Anya shaved a branch down to a point and stuck it in the ground. "Never."

The stone slab door behind the archway on the ground level rose. Tatiana came out, ashen faced.

Zora ran to her. "What happened?"

"I don't know how to say this," Tatiana said. She glanced at Zora, away, then back again. "We've been fooled."

Anya arrived with her sword firm in her grip. "No, *you've* been fooled. Care to explain?"

"I don't know what Gossamer was thinking. He summoned Grey Cloak and Dyphestive into the tower and sent them through the portal."

Zora and Anya exchanged concerned looks.

"And where did he send them? To the past?" Zora asked.

Tatiana swallowed. "I'm ashamed to say, but Gossamer betrayed us. He deceived us." Her jaw clenched. "I can't believe it. He fought with us. I thought he was our friend."

Zora grabbed her friend by the collar. "What did he do with them?"

"As I said, he sent them through the portal. They could be anywhere."

"Didn't Gossamer tell you?" she asked.

"If he won't talk, bring him to me, and I'll squeeze the answer out of him," offered Anya.

"No, Gossamer disappeared after that. Before he departed, he said, 'Long live Black Frost.'" Tatiana hugged Zora. "Dear friend, I am sorry. This is not a matter I could have foreseen."

"Of course not, because you have your head too far up your own—"

"Anya, not now." Zora patted Tatiana on the back. She could feel the other woman's tears on her shoulders. "Be strong. You cannot take all of the blame."

"Of course she can. She is the one who locked all of you out of the tower. It's clearly her responsibility." Anya scoffed. "I told you that you shouldn't have listened to her. I warned you. Yet, here we are again."

"Tatiana, concentrate. Can't we bring them back?" Zora asked.

"No. Gossamer destroyed the Pedestal of Power. And they don't even have this." Tatiana held up the bronze collar that was used to summon her back. "Wherever they are, they are on their own."

Zora broke away from Tatiana then began to massage her own face. Anya was right. It was the second time that the incident in the tower had worked against them. They'd lost the brothers twice. Fatigue assailed her, and she sat. "What are we going to do now?"

Anya said, "We have to move forward the same way we

always did. We shall fight with what we have. There must be more than one way to destroy Black Frost, with or without Dyphestive and Grey Cloak."

Zora continued to stare at the ground. "I suppose that makes you our leader now."

"Well, I..." Tatiana started to say, but when she caught the disapproving looks of her friends, she stopped. "I'll help in any way that I can."

"It might be best if you stayed in the tower."

Razor and Gorva approached.

"What is happening?" Gorva asked.

Zora quickly filled them in.

"We've been through all of this for nothing. I can't believe I'm hearing this," Razor said.

"It isn't for nothing. It's only a setback. With or without our friends, we still have our responsibility to fight Black Frost," Tatiana said. "We've carried on this quest with and without Grey Cloak and Dyphestive before, and we've lost many others along the way. We have to move forward. We will pursue the dragon charms, same as we did before."

"Are you serious?" Zora tossed up her hands. "Black Frost has hundreds of dragon riders, if not a thousand. We'll need to recover hundreds of charms to match them." She opened Crane's satchel. "And so far, we only have one."

"If we find the artifact, the Dragon Helm, it will be a formidable weapon," Tatiana said. She swung her attention to Anya. "And you can train more dragon riders. I know there are people that are willing."

Zora sank her head between her knees. She stank of sweat, and her limbs were exhausted. She didn't care to do anything but go back to Raven Cliff and rest, and the last thing she wanted to hear was her friends squabbling with one another. She'd heard enough. "No one said this would be easy. I'm willing to go after the Dragon Helm. At least try. That's what Grey Cloak and Dyphestive would do." She eyed Anya. "What do you think?"

"My mind has never changed. I wish nothing but to destroy Black Frost at all costs. I'd be happy to lead this quest. Not that I trust that forked tongue of a wizard, but I want to know more about this Dragon Helm."

37

DARK MOUNTAIN

GOSSAMER'S RING teleported him from the Wizard Watch to the base of Black Frost's temple. The icy winds of the gloomy climate cut him to the bone as he stood with his shoes in snow, staring at the massive ziggurat that Black Frost called home. At its base, the temple was over one hundred yards of massive stones perfectly fit together. Small birds nested on the icy ledges. They paid the newcomer no mind.

He pulled his robes tight over his shoulders and began his ascent up the narrow stairs. One step became a hundred. A hundred became a thousand. His thighs ached, and his ankles burned. He flexed his fingers that were stiffening up.

Howling winds tore at his clothing. He took a look down from the platform where the stairs switched back the other way. Jagged teeth of black rock waited to devour him below. Pits of volcanic activity were scattered all over Dark Mountain's rocky climbs. Steam rose toward the gray clouds. The setting was as grim as it was cold. He saw the present. He saw the future.

What have I done?

When Gossamer arrived at the top, his legs were shaking. His teeth clattered, and he couldn't feel his fingers and toes. Black Frost was impossible to miss. The humongous black dragon's body, a mountain of scales bigger than the large shields of men, filled the top of the temple. Warmth emanated from him.

Scores of middling dragons were perched along the outer rim of the temple, their wings folded behind their backs as they faced outward. Like statues, they didn't flinch or move. Snow dressed the horns on their heads.

From his position, it appeared that Gossamer stood at Black Frost's backside. He could see the dragon's great tail curling around his body. He started to walk, following the direction of the tail.

A young elven man approached him, wearing white woolen robes and light-brown hair cut short. His pointed ears were red from long exposure to the cold winds. He politely bowed and said in a pleasant voice, "Hello. I am Datris. And you are?"

"I am Gossamer, a servant from the Wizard Watch. I have urgent news for Black Frost."

"It must be very important if you dared climb to the top of the temple, where death might wait." Datris waved him over. "Please, follow me, Gossamer."

He joined the young elf's side.

"I must say, it has been a long time since I have spoken to another person. I'm glad that we met. I'll be very interested to hear the news that you bring. But I can't appear too interested. Our master would not like that." He led Gossamer down the roof of the temple and pointed at Black Frost's horns. "Isn't he magnificent?"

Gossamer nodded. He'd never seen Black Frost face-to-face. He'd only heard about his mountainous girth. The stories didn't do him justice.

"I will make the introduction. Wait here." Datris disappeared behind the other side of Black Frost's front paw. The talons were enormous in size—one alone was bigger than a horse. Datris reappeared and said, "Come. He will see you, Gossamer. I will be near. I hope your meeting goes well. If not, perhaps I will see you again in the next world."

"Yes, perhaps." Gossamer made his way toward Black Frost. The dragon's head was twenty times larger than Cinder's. His icy-blue eyes were as radiant as the sun. Deep behind the black pupils, an inferno burned within.

"Speak," Black Frost said.

His hot breath melted all of Gossamer's chills away. He bowed and took one knee. Never one to be nervous, he ended up clearing his throat. "Glorious One, the Wizard

Watch in the Wilds is lost. Your servants Dirklen and Magnolia have been banished along with the underlings to another world using the Time Mural. The armies have been routed by a group that calls themselves Talon. They had many dragons with them, the children of Cinder. They were led by the children of Zanna Paydark and Olgstern Stronghair, who go by the names Grey Cloak and Dyphestive."

Black Frost didn't bat a lash.

Gossamer continued, "In your service, I seized an opportunity. Grey Cloak wished to move into the past to destroy you. I deceived him by opening the portal and sending him to another world. To my regret, I had to destroy the ability to use the portals. When I completed my mission, I came here. I am your servant."

The tip of Black Frost's tail started to thump on the top of the temple. His eyes narrowed. "It appears that many have failed me. How can I be certain that you have not failed me as well?"

"Your very existence is proof that you are safe. The sons of Zanna and Olgstern are a threat no longer. Only a small number of fighters remain as your opposition. It won't take any time at all for your superior forces to snuff them out. I'd be glad to lend you my assistance."

"I want control of the Wizard Watch. I want the Time Mural operational and under my full control. Do you understand?"

"Majestic One, the portal is the only viable threat to you. If it were to fall under the control of your enemies, your life would be in peril."

Black Frost inched his face closer. "You will see to it that won't happen. If you refuse, I will find someone who will. Do you understand?"

Gossamer vigorously nodded. He bowed again. "I will do as you command."

"Datris!" Black Frost said. The elf appeared in a moment. "Take him inside the temple and hold him. We need to verify his story. Take him to the Tormentors."

Datris bowed. "As you wish, Glorious One." He took Gossamer by the arm. "Come with me."

38

Grey Cloak sat up, his hands and feet sunk into a snowbank.

Dyphestive was buried headfirst in the same bank, kicking his feet and digging out with his arms. He pushed out of the snow with a pile of it on the top of his head then wiped the ice from his eyes. "Where are we?"

It was daytime, and the skies were clear. "I have no idea," Grey Cloak replied.

Streak popped his head out of the snow. "Hello, brothers." He dug his way out and shook the snow from his body like a hound. His breath was frosty. "Cold climate. Nice change of venue. I like it."

Grey Cloak and Dyphestive stared at Streak then shared a worried glance.

"What?" Streak said. He spun around while inspecting

his body. "Do I have something on me? Is there something in my teeth?" He smiled. "I hate that. And no one ever wants to tell you." He stretched his neck out and eyed them. "Now stop staring at me like I have warts on my horns. What's wrong?"

Grey Cloak stretched out his arms then picked the dragon up.

Streak tilted his head from side to side. His yellow eyes widened suddenly. "Oh... I'm a runt again."

"Perhaps not. Maybe we are giants," Dyphestive said as he stood and brushed the snow from his shoulders. He patted Streak on the head with his shovel-sized hand. "I like you little."

"Sure, what isn't better than a compact dragon?" He clawed at the air. "Put me down, will you? I'm not a baby."

Grey Cloak dropped him. "Sorry, old friend. Maybe it's for the best."

Streak paced. "Best? I'd gotten used to being bigger, and now I'm small." He breathed out smoke. "Not that there is anything wrong with being small, mind you. Small is special," he muttered to himself. "Yeah, special."

"No offense, but we have more important matters to figure out." Absentmindedly, Grey Cloak tightened the Cloak of Legends around his body. No matter what the temperature was like outside, he was always comfortable and cozy inside the cloak. "It appears the sun is setting, and it will be colder soon. We'll all need shelter."

"I'm ready to explore," Dyphestive said. He still wore his chest armor, and his arms were bare. Aside from his buckskin trousers, he didn't have on anything but his boots. "I can go all night and well into tomorrow."

"Of course." Grey Cloak slowly spun around and surveyed the snowy landscape. The snow-covered plains went on for leagues. Clusters of pine trees could be seen in the distance. North, south, east, and west were all fields of snow, but something was very familiar about them. "If we are still in Gapoli, we have to be in the North."

"And if we are in the North, we are close to Dark Mountain," Dyphestive said. "If we are in Gapoli at all."

"Why would you think we aren't in Gapoli?"

Dyphestive shrugged. "I don't know Gossamer as well as you do. Are you certain we could trust him? What if he sent us to another world? A world made of snow."

"Maybe we are the only living things in the snow world too. Well, us and a bunch of cute runt dragons with long eyelashes and pretty scales," Streak said. "We could name it Streak's World."

"We aren't in another world. We are in Gapoli."

"I don't know. I've been to another world before, and this might be that one?" Streak said. He walked along the top of the snow and sniffed. "I smell food. Far away, but it's food, nonetheless. Anyone hungry?"

"I've never missed a meal," Dyphestive said.

"You can say that again." Grey Cloak chuckled and

patted his brother on the back. "Regardless of where we are, I'm glad you are here. I'm glad you are both here, big or small."

Streak spread his wings, started running, then took to the air. He circled around the brothers. "I'll scout and I'll be back in no time."

"Streak, wait." The runt dragon was gone. "Oh, never mind. He'll be fine, I suppose."

"He seems to know more about other worlds than we do. We could use his experience," Dyphestive said.

"I'm telling you, we aren't in another world. Why would Gossamer do that? It serves no purpose."

"It would serve Black Frost's purpose to get us out of the way, permanently."

Grey Cloak shook his head. "No, Gossamer wouldn't do that. I've fought by his side. He risked his life for mine. You weren't there when we fought the hydra."

"Hydra?"

"I didn't tell you that? We fought three of them. The first had four heads, the second five, and the third six."

Dyphestive's face lit up. "I want details!"

Seeing how there wasn't anything else to do, Grey Cloak obliged. "The first one nearly killed us because it took us a while to learn that we had to cut all of its heads off to kill it. Lo and behold, once we kill it, another one comes, and it has five heads. So we know how to kill it, but it's still dangerous."

"That's incredible."

"Gossamer fought valiantly," he added.

"He had to, or you both would have been killed. He's an odd bird. Black and white. Don't you find that suspicious?"

Grey Cloak said, "You are becoming ever insightful."

"I am, aren't I?"

"It's becoming annoying," Grey Cloak joked. "Tell me, what were you and Anya talking about? You appeared to be in an intimate conversation."

Dyphestive's cheeks started to turn rosy. "We talked about our battles. We share the same passion."

"I could see that. Remember the first time you met her? You said you were going to marry her."

"I said that?"

"And now, you don't remember anything." He smirked. "How convenient."

Streak appeared and dropped in the snow before them. His big yellow eyes were wide.

Grey Cloak asked, "What is it?"

"We are traveling with the wind, aren't we?" Streak asked.

Grey Cloak could tell by the movement of his cloak that the wind was behind them. "Obviously. Why?"

"I believe something caught our scent. Something that is hunting."

"Why do you think that?" he asked.

Streak shrugged his wings. "Because I see them with my own two eyes."

"I thought it was one thing. How many did you see?"

"A dozen or so."

Grey Cloak frowned. "A dozen or so what?"

"Snow monsters."

39

GREY CLOAK DREW a sword and handed it to Dyphestive. "What do you mean by 'snow monsters'?" he asked the dragon.

"You know, snow monsters, yetis, uh... Bigfoot." Streak huffed out smoke. "Oversized men bigger than Dyphestive and covered in thick hair."

"Don't exaggerate, Streak. Now isn't the time for jesting." Grey Cloak narrowed his eyes. A light snow was falling, but he didn't see any sign of the snow monsters. "I don't see anything."

Dyphestive flipped the sword end over end. His hand covered the entire pommel. "Small sword."

"It's a long sword. There's nothing small about it. Your hand is too fat for the pommel." Grey Cloak hurried to rise, and the others followed. The clouds in the west were darker, and night began to fall fast. He couldn't see more than fifty yards away. He heard the distant sound of a baying wolf.

Streak's pink tongue flicked out of his mouth. "Oh, and there is a wolf too."

More wolves began to bay.

"I meant wolves," Streak added as his tail tapped on the snow. "Did I mention they are big?"

The Rod of Weapons ignited. Grey Cloak said, "We can handle wolves, surely?"

"And snow monsters. Don't forget about the snow monsters." Streak scratched his earhole with his front paw. "I wonder if they will melt if I use my breath on them."

"Perhaps you should douse your light," Dyphestive suggested.

"I'm hoping it will scare them."

The baying wolves fell silent.

"See?" Grey Cloak said. "They are frightened and flee."

The icy winds picked up and tore at their clothing. They remained in position, watching the plains.

"Something comes," Dyphestive said.

"I told you," Streak replied.

A large figure of a man lingered near one of the snow-banks. He appeared to have a club of some sort in his hand. "He's big," Grey Cloak said. "Very big. Perhaps we can frighten him." He aimed the rod at the creatures.

"That might provoke them," Streak mentioned.

"True, but they are hunting us, anyway. If we can frighten them off, it's all for the better." He fired a blue ball of fire over the monster's head.

It let out a savage roar and beat its chest.

"I think you should have hit him. That only made him mad," Dyphestive said.

"It can't hurt to try." Grey Cloak fired another ball of energy. It sped over the snowy landscape and blasted into the snow monster's body. It fell out of sight. Grey Cloak craned his neck. "That might have done it."

"I don't hear the wolves howling anymore," Streak said. He tilted his head in quick movements like a bird. He rolled out his tongue and caught a snowflake. "Mmm... tasty."

Grey Cloak walked east. "Let's take a closer look and see what we are up against. Perhaps I killed it."

Streak walked on top of the snow, thanks to the webbing between his talons. "I told you, there are many that I saw."

"We are out in the wild. Whatever they are won't be used to seeing magic. Primitive people are terrified of such elements." Grey Cloak took his time. His eyes darted from side to side, searching for any unnatural movement. They covered the distance. Very large footprints marked the snow.

Dyphestive took a knee and put his oversized hand inside the print. "That's one big, hairy man. Or monster. It has a stink too."

"I think that's burnt hair from where I hit it," Grey Cloak said.

"You mean fur," Streak said.

"Yes, if you want to be precise, we'll call it fur. Are you happy?"

"I'm always happy," Streak said. "I might be a little happier than I was a moment earlier, but to be clear, I was happy already."

Grey Cloak patted his dragon's head. "Good to know." He spun the staff around but kept the mystic light burning. "Whatever it was, I believe we scared it off. I seriously doubt that it will come within fifty yards of us anymore. Not if it knows what is good for it." He looked at his friends. "Shall we proceed?"

"After you." Dyphestive managed a clumsy sword spin. "I miss the iron sword. Using a smaller sword will take some getting used to."

"I'm sure you will manage," he replied.

"I need a bigger handle. This longsword is fitted for a smaller hand. Like yours. Tiny."

"I don't have small hands."

"Well, you don't have big ones."

Grey Cloak lifted his palm and turned it from side to side. "Yes, I do. Yours are unnaturally enormous. Can we change the subject?"

"To what?"

"Oh, I don't know. Perhaps we need to focus on figuring

out where we are. Once again, assuming we are in Gapoli, we have to be north. Either south of the Dark Ridges or north of them. That is the only thing that I can think of."

"They do have snow in other worlds," Streak said.

"I'm not going to journey down that road." He rubbed his jaw. "South."

"What?" Dyphestive said.

"South. We should go south. If we are in Gapoli, we will run into the Dark Ridges if we are north of them. If we are south of them, we will walk into the Northern territory of Westerlund." He shrugged. "It might be a lot of walking, but it will be easy."

Dyphestive nodded. "You believe we are in Ice Vale?"

"It's the only logical conclusion. Chances are, we'll be able to see more in the morning." He turned south.

The wolves renewed their baying. In the distance, towering men rose from the snow and surrounded the heroes in all directions.

"I TOLD you there were a lot of them. I told you," Streak said.

Grey Cloak made a quick count as he turned his head over his shoulders.

"I count fourteen, and that isn't including the wolves," Dyphestive said. He tapped the flat of his blade in the palm of his hand. "I've never fought an enemy like this before. They look big enough to rip your arms off with their bare hands."

The snow monsters crept closer, slowly collapsing their circle on them from all directions. Each and every one of them was over seven feet tall, a mound of furry muscle. Many of them clutched crude clubs in their hands, but some carried nothing at all. Wolves escorted every other one, the hackles on their backs coming up to the snow monsters' knees.

"It looks like we walked right into their trap," Streak commented. "I tried to warn you."

"We didn't have much choice, regardless." There was no mistaking the hungry look in the shambling men's faces. They wanted food. They wanted blood. He reached into his inner pockets and pulled out the Figurine of Heroes. "It looks like I am going to have to try to even the odds."

"I thought you gave the figurine back to Tatiana," Dyphestive said with a raised brow.

"Heh—she thought so too." He dropped the figurine on the ground before him and said, "Please don't be underlings. Please don't be underlings." He chanted the mystic word, "*Osid-ayan-umra-shokrah-ha!*"

The figurine began to smolder and spit smoke. The plume of smoke spread.

Grey Cloak and Dyphestive backed away a few steps.

The snow monsters stopped in their tracks.

A half dozen shadowy figures appeared inside the inky depths of the clearing smoke. The wind took the last rolls of smoke away. A rugged-looking band of well-armored warriors stood in the snow. Towering among them was another snow-monster type with chestnut fur. He had a weapon strapped over his shoulder like the one that the man called Smoke had carried in the battle at Monarch Castle.

"Say, an M-60 machine gun. A nice piece of hardware. I like our odds better already," Streak said.

"What gives?" the shaggy creature said as he looked down at Grey Cloak.

"We need a hand." He pointed at the snow monsters.

"You want me to kill troglins like me?" the shaggy man said.

"Easy, Solomon. I'll handle this." The soldier wore breastplate armor with a crown engraved in the metal. His hair was jet black, his beard neatly trimmed. His piercing eyes saw into the soul, and his chin was hard as iron. He carried a heavy length of steel in his hand. "I'm Ruger Slade. You summoned me and the Henchmen." He eyed the snow monsters. "I take it they are a problem."

Grey Cloak nodded.

Ruger nodded. "We are their problem now." He patted Grey Cloak on the shoulder. "We will aid you, pointy-eared one." He glanced at Dyphestive. "Young fella, you need a bigger sword with a body like that."

"I know," Dyphestive replied.

"Horace," Ruger said to a rough-looking man with a full beard and a spear with a large head, "you and Bearclaw defend the east." He took command as he chopped his arm, section by section. "Solomon, lay down a suppressing line of fire starting in the north."

"You know I don't like killing. I told you I don't like killing," Solomon whined as he pulled the charging handle of his weapon. "Always killing. I'm a hippy. We bring peace."

"Fine. Let them eat you, then. Or use that big gun and follow orders." Ruger addressed a handsome blond with curly hair who stood nearby. "Vern, shoulder to shoulder with me in the west." He dropped his gaze to a husky woman with a cute pie face and a twinkle in her eye. She was dressed in olive-colored robes. "Iris, keep with these young men and defend the south. Use your spells."

Iris slapped Dyphestive on the rear end. "I'd be happy to. What is your name, young fella?"

"Dyphestive."

"Nice to meet you." She gave him the once-over. "Very nice indeed." She pulled a small vial from her pocket. "Let me see that blade." She rubbed an oily substance on it. The sword's steel burst into flame. "Ah, that's what you call an attention getter."

Ruger Slade raised his commanding voice. "Remember our creed, Henchmen!"

Every one of his men shouted back, "Death before failure!"

The snow monsters came with their slavering jaws opened wide and their clubs hoisted over their heads.

"Great." Fire blasted out of the barrel of Solomon's machine gun. Bullets filled a snow monster's chest and sent it to the ground, bleeding.

The startled snow monsters slowed the moment their companion dropped. Their wild calls turned into rage.

"We made them mad." Solomon blasted away. "I can feel the negativity. It's really ruined my peaceful vibe."

Grey Cloak shot fireballs out of his staff.

Streak took flight.

Dyphestive stepped up with the flaming sword in his grip.

Iris hurled a small jug that exploded underneath the paws of a charging wolf.

The Henchmen engaged fully.

Grey Cloak caught the surrounding action out of the corner of his eye. Ruger Slade ran into a snow monster and disemboweled the beast in a blink of an eye. He spun away and chopped off a second monster's arm at the elbow. He drove steel into the same beast's heart.

Horseshoes! These men can fight!

The savage snow monsters fought with ravenous ferocity. Clubs made of hip bones went up and came down. The bearded one, Horace, took a club to the chest. Vern slipped underneath the weight of a snow-furred goon. It hammered him with fists. Wolves tore at his legs.

The Henchmen were in a bind. They were losing.

41

Streak flew over the heads of the snow monsters while singing a song:

"The weather outside is frightful...

The monsters are not delightful...

But since we have no place to go, let it snow, let it snow... fireballs."

He spit out a stream of flames that engulfed a snow monster and a wolf then resumed singing.

"You're a mean one, Mister Streak..."

A wolf leapt upward, nipped at his legs, then dropped back into the snow.

"Mush! Mush! You mangy cur!"

He spit and turned the dog into a running, yelping pillar of fire. He glided out above the fracas, turned his neck, and caught a rock with his face. He dropped from the sky and was buried in the snow.

One of the snow monsters pulled him out of the frosty heap and forced him into his big mouth.

"Solomon! What are you doing? Start shooting holes in these bloody things!" Ruger ordered. He ducked under the monsters' crushing arms and sank his sword deep into the creature's belly.

The snow monster howled. Its fists came down on the armored plates covering Ruger's shoulders. He fell into the snow. He clawed at the ground while the snow monsters started to drag him away. He caught Grey Cloak's glance. "Don't worry. The longer we fight, the better we get."

Facing the surging enemy, Grey Cloak couldn't help but think, *We don't have longer. They'll vanish at any moment.* With a handful of the snow monsters down, he redoubled his efforts. Using his speed, he ducked from the clutch of one snow monster and buried the Rod of Weapons in the back of another. He spun before the monster turned around and smote him deep in the ribs.

Two wolves converged on them from opposite directions. He jumped high. The wolves' skulls met and clacked together.

The Cloak of Legends held Grey Cloak aloft. During his slow descent, he fired the rod's missile weapon into the wolves. They ran away, yelping, their bodies on fire.

Four down. Zooks, how many more to go?

A snow monster crept behind him, grabbed his cloak, and yanked him to the ground.

Dyphestive cut a wolf's head off on the way to fight a snow monster.

It attacked him with a wooden club then lifted its arms and held the club overhead.

He pierced it in the chest with the longsword.

The club smashed down on his skull. White stars exploded in his eyes. The next thing he knew, he was on his hands and knees. He looked up.

The snow monster ripped the sword out of its chest and flung it away. It used the club and pounded Dyphestive with one hand.

He rolled to his back and grabbed the snow monster's wrists. It put its full weight on him and screamed in his face. Saliva dripped from its rotting teeth, and the smell was rank. Dyphestive pushed the monster back. The knots in his arms bulged. He pulled his knee back and kicked it in the crotch.

"Gurk!" the snow monster said.

Dyphestive smashed his skull into the monster's nose.

They rolled over the snow. Dyphestive locked his fingers on the snow monster's neck. It dug its fingernails into his. They screamed as they tried to squeeze the life out of each other.

The full weight of the snow monster fell upon Grey Cloak, crushing him in the suffocating snow. He wormed his way out from underneath the monster that lay on him, unmoving. He popped out from under it to find a grizzly warrior with a broad, clean-shaven face and hawkish features rip a battle axe out of the dead snow monster's skull. "Thank you," Grey Cloak said.

The warrior hooked him under the arm and helped him to his feet. "Bearclaw is glad to help." He set his restless eyes on a new enemy and took off.

Grey Cloak caught the blond-haired warrior, Vern, climbing out from beneath another snow monster. He wiped snow from his eyes, but another snow monster approached him, its club high, ready to crush his skull. "Vern! Watch out!"

Vern looked up in time to see the club starting to come down.

The broad blade of a spear burst from the front of the monster's chest. Its club fell from its hands, still stretched overhead, and bounced off its skull. The spear vanished as quickly as it had appeared. It fell face-first into the snow, and Vern jumped away.

Horace stood on the other side, snow-monster blood dripping from his spear. "Quit falling down, Vern, and help us kill something!"

"I killed the one that fell on me!" Vern said. He retrieved his blade and spun it with his wrist. "I'll kill more than you before the day is done."

Streak gave the snow monster what it wanted. He pushed his face all the way into the monster's jaws until his nose reached the back of its throat. "You want me, you got me." Streak let out his flame. The dragon fire turned the monster's guts into jelly. He cooked the foul beast from the inside out.

In a final desperate effort, the snow monster yanked Streak free of its jaws. Smoke poured out of its eyes and ears. It wandered across the snow and collapsed.

"Now that's cookin'," Streak said.

Dyphestive's iron grip held. The monster's did not. He pushed his fingers deeper into the monster's throat.

It broke its grip and tore its claws into Dyphestive's back, but the strength went out of its body. It let out a ragged gasp and died.

A wolf charged into Dyphestive's blind side. A small jar exploded on the wolf then caught fire.

Iris waded toward him with her robes hiked up and her feet kicking up the snow. With a warm smile on her face, she said, "You have nasty scrapes on your back. I need to take your jerkin off so I can take a closer look at you—your back, I mean. Oh, who am I fooling?"

Ruger Slade cut through the wrists of the monster towing him through the snow. He sat up quickly and jabbed the sword into the monster's throat. It ran off, bleeding, made it a few dozen yards, and fell into the snow.

The monsters and wolves were routed, the snowy fields were bathed in blood, and a steady snowfall began to quickly cover the stained field.

Ruger cleaned his sword in the snow and said to Grey Cloak, "A fine battle. I'm glad we could aid you in your moment of distress."

"Not as glad as we are." Grey Cloak offered his hand. "I hope my summoning didn't ruin your life."

"No, not hardly at all. We could always use a break from doing the king's dirty work." Ruger nodded at Solomon. Smoke streamed from the hairy monster's gun barrel. "I see you've been busy."

Solomon shook his head. "I need to get away from you and get back to my world and my body."

"Tell us more about your world," Grey Cloak prompted.

"Our world is called Titanuus, and what is the name of this pla—" Ruger's voice deteriorated into silence as the Henchmen's bodies started to fade into smoke. He used his sword to salute and gave them a final nod before entering back into the figurine.

42

Grey Cloak and Dyphestive made a camp near where they fought. They skinned a few wolves, and Dyphestive tied them into a bundle.

"I'll make a vest out of them." He warmed his hands over a wood fire that Streak had started, and they cooked wolf meat on sticks. "I wonder what the snow monsters taste like."

"Don't even think about it. They are people," Grey Cloak said.

"They didn't seem like people."

"Agreed," Streak said, "but I'd still eat them. Dragons eat anything. We might not have tried anything, but we'll eat anything. Well, not rocks, metal, or glass, but you get the idea."

Grey Cloak huddled in front of the fire, holding the

Figurine of Heroes in the palm of his hands. It had saved them again.

Dyphestive used his bundle of pelts as a chair, sat, and began to gnaw on his meat on a stick. "Chewy but palatable. What's on your mind? Aren't you glad you used the figurine? I am. We might not have lasted otherwise."

Grey Cloak smoothed a hand over the figurine's glassy surface. "I'm glad I did what I did. No regrets on my end. It's good to know you don't have any regrets, either. It's exhilarating to use it without hearing Tatiana's complaining."

"We may not hear her complaints ever again, at the rate we are going."

"Wouldn't that be nice? But for some sad reason, I can't shake her voice out of my head." He placed the figurine back inside one of his many pockets. "Hopefully, we won't have need of it again anytime soon."

"The longer the better, but I enjoy the fighting." Dyphestive swallowed a mouthful. "Aren't you going to eat?"

Grey Cloak saw Streak helping himself. "Why not?" He grabbed a hunk from the spit and gave it a try. "Not bad. It's not chicken, but a man can live off of it."

"Why don't the pair of you get some rest?" Streak suggested. "I'll keep watch, since I'm not prone to sleeping."

"You sleep all the time," Dyphestive said.

"You're right. You take watch, and I'll sleep." Streak nuzzled into the snow, curled his tail around his body, and closed his eyes.

"We should leave him," Dyphestive joked.

"I heard that. Just because my eyelids are closed doesn't mean my earholes aren't open." Streak stuck his tongue out and appeared to go to sleep.

"I know you're tired, brother. Let me take the first watch," Dyphestive said.

Grey Cloak yawned, which was a rarity. "I don't think I'll be able to sleep, but after I finish my dinner, I'll try."

Grey Cloak awoke the next morning with the sensation of Streak shoveling snow in his face. "Will you quit that?" He sat up and cleared his blurry eyes. The snowy hills were bathed in bright sun, which shone in his eyes. He searched out Dyphestive, who was covering the campfire with snow. "Why didn't you wake me sooner? I needed to take watch."

Streak raised his wing. "I can answer that. I woke your anvil-headed brother before I woke you. He was snoring like a baby."

"Is that true?"

Dyphestive nodded. "Sorry. I don't know what overcame me. It happened."

"We are all exhausted. I can't blame you. We need to be glad that nothing crept up on us." He rose and stretched his back. The skies were pale blue, without a cloud to be seen. "We'll continue south."

Dyphestive picked up the bundle, and Streak took to the sky. "I'll scout ahead."

"Streak! Oh, never mind. He didn't listen the last time, and he won't listen this time, either." He started through the snow with the stiff wind in his face. "Why don't you take the lead?"

"Gladly." Dyphestive bulled his way south, flattening a path in the ankle-deep snow. They walked league after league, one hour after another. "When we get somewhere, I hope they have a tavern, a bed, and a warm fire. I miss the simple things."

"Agreed." Grey Cloak searched the skies. He hadn't seen Streak in hours. It was something he'd gotten used to over the years, but something felt different. He recalled the time he and Anya were in Loose Boot and Streak had been stolen. It left him with an unsettling feeling.

He was small then too.

43

THE DARK RIDGES appeared on the southern horizon after two days of traveling through the cold. There was no mistaking the spiny, snowcapped peaks that pierced the clouds. Fields of blue pines were nestled at the mountain range's base.

Grey Cloak breathed a sigh of relief. Though the base of the mountains was still leagues and hours of walking away, at least he knew he was home. "I believe I see smoke ahead," he said to Dyphestive.

Dyphestive stood with a bundle of wolf fur on his shoulder and sniffed. "I think you are right. Where there is fire, there is food and company." He eyed the mountains. "Are you sure they are the Dark Ridges? How can you know for certain?"

"I can tell by the peaks. I distinctly remember them

from when Anya and I spent time in Loose Boot." He pointed at a pair of mountain peaks. "Those two right there are called the Bull's Horns. The locals were talking about them. They are the tallest along the range." The clouds had passed over the Bull's Horns, covering their tips again. "It's them."

Dyphestive nodded. "I'll take your word for it, brother."

Streak returned for the second time in as many days with a rabbit in his mouth. He landed, dropped the white-eared bunny, and watched it hop away. "Isn't he cute? We've been playing all morning, but I keep scaring the pellets out of him."

"Aside from seeing more varmints, did you notice anything else that might be helpful?" Grey Cloak asked.

Streak scratched his earhole with his back paw like a dog. "I made it as far as the mountains' base. Men and dwarves are timbering. The pines are coming down. They appear to be cutting up the logs and heading west along the base." Streak searched for the rabbit. "That little dickens thinks he's going to get away. We'll see about that." He took flight then sped after the frightened rabbit.

"The lumberjacks should be able to shed some light on our situation." Grey Cloak bowed then stepped aside. "After you."

They arrived at the lumberjack camp not long before dusk. Well-built men dressed in furs, wool, and buckskin chopped branches off of trees. They chained up the logs then rolled them onto large sleds pulled northwest by a team of horses.

Together, they walked along the trail in the snow. Not a single one of the rough-hewn men paid them any mind. They sank their axes into the trees with their brawny shoulders covered in snow.

"Follow the food. Where there is food, there are people. They talk more when they aren't hungry," Dyphestive said.

"Did you get enough wolf meat?"

"I never have enough to eat. I'm still growing."

"Ha." Grey Cloak had to bear in mind that he and his brother had only seen about eighteen or nineteen seasons of life, though it seemed a lot longer. "I guess you could still be growing. Too bad for food."

They found a small camp made of several small log cabins. There was a fire in the center, surrounded by stones. Dead deer lay on the ground, and a pair of dwarves cooked food over the fire, assisted by three halfling women. The dwarves' woolen beards were gray, and one of them was missing an eye. He stood on the stones, stirring a long ladle inside a metal pot that hung over the fire. He sipped from the ladle when he noticed the brothers.

"Keep moving," the dwarf said in a harsh voice. "If you aren't chopping wood, I'm not feeding you. This isn't a charity."

The cute halfling women wearing winter garb giggled and hurried into one of the nearby cabins.

Grey Cloak cautiously approached the dwarves. "Pardon us. We aren't looking for food. We only wish to know what year it is?"

The dwarves could have been twin brothers—it was hard to tell. Both of them were missing the same eye, but the one sawing horns off of the deer had a darker beard.

The one with the gray beard said, "What do you mean, 'what year is it?' A dwarf lives, and a dwarf dies. We have better ways to spend our time than counting the days. Oysh!" He glanced at the furs. "Those are very nice pelts. What are you asking for them?"

Dyphestive rubbed his jaw. "I could part with one for some food and shelter for my brother and me."

The dwarves stood beside each other and looked past Dyphestive, their stares following the trail in the snow. "Is your brother far behind? If he's big like you, we'll need two pelts."

"No." Dyphestive dropped his hand onto Grey Cloak's shoulder. "This is my brother. My blood brother."

"Oh. That's strange, but we've seen stranger things than men and elves calling themselves brothers." The gray beard checked out Grey Cloak and said, "We don't have greens here. Only grains and beef. Can you make a meal of that, elf?"

"I like beef. I'll eat all that you serve me."

"Good, because that is all that you'll be getting. Toss me that pelt."

Dyphestive obliged.

The dwarven men ran their hands over the fur. The gray beard put it over his shoulders, and the pelt covered them. His comrade wrapped his around his chest to check the size.

"This is a large wolf you killed. A real howler. How'd you kill so many of them? They are vicious," the gray beard said.

"We are good hunters," Grey Cloak said.

"You don't look like hunters," the man replied. The other dwarf didn't appear to be interested at all. "You look like fish out of water to me." He examined the pelt, and his good brow furrowed. "Howlers are the yettins' pets. Did you happen to hunt down the yettins too?"

Grey Cloak shrugged. "Maybe."

44

ON THE VERY SAME NIGHT, the lumberjacks gathered around the fire and listened to Grey Cloak tell the story about their battle with the yettins. The gathering consisted of simple folk with skin as tough as leather and eyes as hard as iron. They lived and breathed logging. It was their life, and they would have had it no other way. It was hard work for durable people who thrived in the cold and the wild.

Smoking from pipes and spitting tobacco juice, they clung to every syllable of Grey Cloak's words. Their eyes filled with shock and amazement while they gobbled down hot venison and washed it down with warm cider.

"I can't believe it. I can't believe it," the gray-bearded dwarf said. He'd finally introduced himself as Hannibull. His son, Hektor, who had a darker beard, sat beside him. They eagerly pounded their fists on their knees. "Tell the part where your brother choked the yettin to death with his bare fingers. That's a dragon of a story!"

"Aye! Aye!" a voice called.

Grey Cloak quenched his dry throat with warm, spicy cider and said to his brother, "Care to take a crack at it? Perhaps your version is better. I might have missed something."

Streak dropped from the sky and landed at Grey Cloak's feet.

The lumberjacks let out audible gasps. Every eye fastened on Streak, and calloused hands snatched up their hatchets.

"Easy, men." Grey Cloak picked up Streak and cradled him in his arms. He whispered, "You really know how to make an entrance. Keep your beak shut and don't startle them." He raised his voice. "This is my dragon, the one who turned the yettin and their howlers into flames. His name is Streak. He won't harm you."

The lumberjacks exchanged wary glances. Many of them hurried into the darkness or vanished into their cabins. It wasn't long before most of the audience was gone.

"You spooked them," Hannibull said. He stuffed more tobacco into his pipe then puffed on the stem. "Dragons are not creatures that we take in. They give us trouble from time to time. Not wee ones like yours, but many consider them a bad omen."

"A good thing for us is that we are only passing

through." Grey Cloak let Streak slip into his hood. "The last thing we want to do is create a stir in front of your people."

"You've already done that. But no worries." Hannibull pointed to one of the cabins. "Take your stay in there. The halflings prepared it for you. I imagine you need rest from your battle. In the morning, we'll supply you, and you can take your journey to Ice Vale's township. You'll find the answers you seek there. After all, we are simple folk. Not ones for all of the clamor and celebrating. It's only two days north of here."

"Thank you, Hannibull," Grey Cloak said.

"Yes, thank you," Dyphestive added.

They entered the small cabin, which barely had enough room for the both of them. Smelly old blankets padded the floor.

Grey Cloak lay down and rested comfortably in his cloak.

Dyphestive covered up in several furs. He yawned loudly, stretched out until his knuckles hit the wall, and said, "Do we want to go to Ice Vale? Or should we go south?"

"Huh—I was thinking the same thing. I find it hard to believe they don't know what year it is. Seems strange. But I think we should go into Ice Vale's township. It will be the best way to find out what year it is."

Wind whistled through the cracks of the small, gloomy room.

"What if we went forward another ten years?" Dyphestive asked.

"Then we would probably be better off living out the rest of our lives in Ice Vale. It will be safer. The sages say the edge of the world always is."

They awoke early the next day to the commotion of angry voices. The lumberjacks had gathered outside and were in a heated discussion.

Grey Cloak and Dyphestive wandered into the camp and tracked down Hannibull and Hektor. The father and son were hurrying down the log route heading east along the base of the mountain. "What's wrong, Hannibull?" Grey Cloak asked.

"Word came that one of our camps was attacked last night. It happens, but this one sounds particularly bad," Hannibull said. He and his son each carried a hand axe. "I need to survey the damage. I hope it isn't as bad as they say it is. The men tend to get excited and exaggerate."

"Can we lend you a hand?" Grey Cloak asked.

"No, this is our business. I know you boys have matters to attend to. I don't want to hold you up," Hannibull said. "But many thanks."

"Yes, good to meet you." Grey Cloak stopped while

Hannibull and Hektor hurried along on their trek. "I suppose they'll be fine."

Streak popped his head out over Grey Cloak's shoulder. "Is it morning? I thought I smelled morning. What is going on?"

"The lumberjacks had some unwanted visitors last night. Not our concern." He turned and almost walked into Dyphestive, who walled him off. "What's his problem?"

"We need to go with them," Dyphestive said. "What if yettin attacked them? That might have been instigated by us."

"You and your insight." Grey Cloak turned around. "Fine, come along."

They followed the dwarves to another lumberjack camp over a league away. Huge log-carrying sleds were flipped over like toys. Several small cabins were smashed to bits. Many, both man and dwarf, were dead. A horse had been half eaten, and its head was missing.

"What could have done this?" Grey Cloak asked as he approached Hannibull.

The dwarf gazed at a huge bloody footprint in the snow. "I know who did this. White Ice did this."

45

———

"WHITE ICE IS an ettin who has been haunting these hills since before I was born. He's a terror. Comes and does as he pleases." Hannibull stood inside the monster's footprint. "Big, he is. Much bigger than the yettin. He'll eat them too. It is a sad day when he comes. Many die. Work is delayed. The merchant's gold is lost."

The barefoot print in the snow was ten times bigger than Grey Cloak's. He marveled at the size. He'd seen giants before on Gunder Island, and White Ice appeared to be as big as any of them. "Hasn't anyone tried to kill him?"

"Oh, believe me, the merchants have tried. Vengeful loved ones have tried. All have failed." He pointed at the mountainside. "Look at those hills. They are massive. Even a creature as big as White Ice is a gnat inside them. But he knows every inch. Better than anything living. That is why he is so hard to track—it makes him impossible to catch. And if you do find him by chance, he'll destroy you."

The lumberjacks began stacking the dead nearby. Men, women, and children's bodies were mangled and crushed.

"We have to stop him," Dyphestive uttered.

Grey Cloak shot him a look. "Not that I don't want to help, but this situation appears to be beyond our control, brother."

Dyphestive stared at the black hills. "We will find him. We will kill him."

"Brother, again, at the risk of sounding impolite, this is not our cause or purpose."

"How many have died over the years because of White Ice?" Dyphestive asked.

"Scores of our kind have fallen over the generations. Scores more will perish over time, but they do it for their families. They do it for the gold." Hannibull clawed at his beard. "I don't blame you for not wanting to put your necks out on account of us. Plenty have tried to help, and all of them have died. This is our life. We chose it. We know the risk involved. Being a lumberjack is a dangerous craft, but that is our craft. We are not warriors and adventurers but peaceful family men."

"That's reason enough for me," Dyphestive said.

Grey Cloak tried to pull his brother aside by the arm, but Dyphestive wouldn't budge. He turned to the dwarves. "Will you pardon us for a spell?"

The dwarves walked away.

"Listen to me. I understand that you want to save everyone. But we can't. We have to focus on the future and stopping Black Frost. If we die, who will stop him then? Huh?"

Dyphestive's jaws clenched. His stare remained fixed on the hills. "We have to do good where we can. We must try."

"We are going into the monster's territory. And big as he may be, it will be like searching for a needle in a haystack." He swung his arm toward the mountain range. "We don't know what horrors lurk in the nooks and crags. There could be anything. Did you ever think what would happen if it traps us?"

"We have the Figurine of Heroes."

"Now you're starting to think like me. That's scary." He shook his head in disappointment and sighed. "I see you won't change your mind. And I tried reasoning."

"You tried well," Streak said.

Grey Cloak called for Hannibull. "We'll give it a go."

Hannibull's and Hektor's solemn expressions brightened. "You mean it?" Hannibull asked.

"We do."

"If you do this, you'll not only find great favor with our camp, but the merchants will reward you as well. I swear upon my pickaxe." Hannibull slapped his son on the back. "Hah! Come with us, heroes. Perhaps we have something that will aid you on your quest."

They went back to the original camp, where the

brothers had slept. Hannibull took them to a blacksmith shop built of heavy timber. A grimy dwarf and a sweaty young man were rounding out horseshoes on separate anvils.

It instantly brought back memories of their days working for Rhonna back in Havenstock, where all of the adventure started. The hard hammering of metal on metal made Grey Cloak's teeth tingle.

Dyphestive had a warm smile on his face.

"Back here! Back here," Hannibull stated as he waved them deeper inside the forge. Heavy tools hung on the walls and were stacked up in the corners. His son climbed the stairs to a loft overhead. Hannibull rummaged through the tools and scrap and hollered, "Hektor, look for a weapon. A big one."

Metal rattled against metal. Wood scraped on steel.

Hannibull slung heavy strips of steel and wooden beams out of his way. "I know it is here. It's been a long time, but it is here. I swear it." He scratched his beard. "Of course, it has been several seasons. Many of them."

"We have weapons, Hannibull," Grey Cloak said. "They'll be adequate."

"Adequate! You've never seen White Ice, but I have. I was a boy, young, wandering in the snow. I saw him. Yes, I did, and his stare turned my bones to ice. He spared me that day. I don't know why—perhaps his belly was filled. Trust me when I say you'll need a weapon... A weapon made here long ago by a warrior who swore to protect us then disappeared into the sky. I never knew his name." He shrugged. "Well, that is what the legends say."

Hektor dropped something long, wrapped in sackcloth, and covered in dust out of the rafters.

"Oh, this is it, I believe. I saw it once, long ago. Many seasons," Hannibull said. He started cutting the cords that bound it with a small knife. "It takes a large man. A very large man has to wield this mighty weapon."

"You've seen a lot of things once, haven't you?" Grey Cloak commented. He gave his brother a doubtful look.

"I don't forget what I see. I forget nothing. Your faces will always be familiar to me." Hannibull rolled the sackcloth away. "See, here it is, a great weapon."

Dyphestive gasped.

Streak flicked his tongue.

Grey Cloak couldn't believe his own eyes. "It is the iron sword."

"Yes, that is what the warrior called it," Hannibull said. "The Iron Sword."

Dyphestive picked it up by the handle and gazed at it with great admiration. He gave his brother an incredulous look and rested the flat of the blade against his forehead. "It's the genuine article, aside from the gem."

46

A CHILLING FEELING raced through Grey Cloak's gut the moment he saw the sword. They might not be trapped in the past but in the future. A hundred scenarios raced through his head.

"Do you like it?" Hannibull asked.

An easy smile crossed Dyphestive's face. "I already feel like it is an old friend." He made a short chop with the sword. "Ha! Plenty big enough to handle an ettin with. I'll cut his head off with one stroke."

"Ettins have two heads," Hannibull said.

"Oh... then it will take two mighty strokes!" Dyphestive marched outside and started practicing with the Iron Sword. His large hands filled the long grip, and he stabbed it at the air.

"We'll need supplies," Grey Cloak said to Hannibull. "I don't imagine this journey will be a short trip."

"No, I wouldn't imagine that, either, but there is life in the mountains. It's scarce, but it is there." Hannibull guided Grey Cloak out of the smithy with a push of his hand. "Come. I'll set you up with all I can. And remember, if you kill the ettin, bring proof. The merchants will need to see it, and it will lift the spirits of our men."

"What do you mean, *if* we kill it?" Grey Cloak looked at the mountain. "We aren't coming back empty-handed."

Hannibull nodded. "Good. I like your determination. I pray you succeed where so many others have failed."

The blood brothers began the trek up into the Dark Ridges at the last spot where the ettin White Ice had last been seen. It wasn't difficult to find the giant's tracks going straight up the hills. Broken branches and crushed saplings had been left in the monster's wake.

Dyphestive towed a small sled behind him, and Streak rode on top of the gear. His twin tails drummed on the wolf pelts as he caught snowflakes with his tongue and sang strange songs.

An absentminded Grey Cloak brought up the rear as he listlessly walked behind them. He couldn't have cared less about the ettin. He was far more concerned about the appearance of the Iron Sword.

"Someone is very quiet," Dyphestive said with a look over his shoulder. "I'd be curious to know what is rattling around in that skull of yours."

"The same thing that should be rattling around in your skull. Where did the Iron Sword come from? That is what." Grey Cloak ducked under a pine branch. "Do you remember the Ruins of Thannis, where we found the Figurine of Heroes, the Rod of Weapons, and the Iron Sword? And here it is again. How can that be?"

"I've been wondering about that too. I consider it to be a blessing to have it in hand, and I don't want to overthink it. Perhaps someone left it there for us?" Dyphestive said.

"How can that be? Who would possibly know where we are going to be if we haven't been there before?" He pushed another low branch away from his face. "It makes me wonder if any of this is real at all."

Dyphestive gave him a curious look. "What do you mean?"

"I don't know what I mean. That's what I mean." Grey Cloak tried to mask his agitation and added, "Do you ever feel as if you are living in a dream?"

"No."

"I do," Streak said. "I dream all the time. There are cute little pink dragons in my dreams, with white wings and beautiful eyes. They eat butterflies." He flicked his tongue and ate a snowflake. "Can I scout now?"

"No!" Grey Cloak sighed. "Sorry, Streak. Be patient. I need to get a message into my brother's thick skull." He caught up to Dyphestive. "We need to move off this hunt. It is a waste of time. The lumberjacks won't know what happened to us. They'll only suspect we are dead. It's time to move on to Ice Vale, where we can figure out where we are. This is urgent, brother."

Dyphestive stopped and looked up the rocky hills. "No. You can't say for certain that this isn't what we are meant to do. Finding the sword is a sign that this is where we are supposed to be, and this is what we should be doing. I can't explain it, either, but that is my gut feeling."

Grey Cloak massaged his temples with his fingers. "You are making my skull ache. All because you want to kiss an ettin."

"I don't want to kiss it."

"No, of course not." Grey Cloak fell behind the sled. He knew all too well how obstinate Dyphestive could be. There wasn't any point in spending more energy trying to change his mind. He caught Streak's bright-yellow eyes fastened on him. "Go ahead and scout, but don't go too far."

Streak stood on his hind legs and saluted with his front paw. "Thank you, sir!"

47

GREY CLOAK COVERED HIS NOSE. "Well done, brother. You've found the most delightful stink."

They'd spent one day and one night in the mountains. It was midday, and they stood inside the large opening of a cave. The trail to find the ettin had gone cold. There were no more footprints or broken branches. It was as if the monster had vanished into the icy air.

Dyphestive dragged the sled deeper inside the cave. He craned his neck as he scanned the rock ceiling, sniffing the air. "Dung. Something has recently paid a visit here."

Grey Cloak eased his way inside while pinching his nose. "Shew! It's making my eyes water." The cave was more than big enough for a giant to enter. The opening was over twenty feet tall and three times as deep. He fed energy into the Rod of Weapons, and a warm blue light blossomed on the end. "What's that you are looking at?"

Dyphestive shielded his nose with a forearm. "I believe it's ettin dung. What a pile—it's as big as a grand dragon's."

"Ew!" Grey Cloak exclaimed. They both knew too much about dragon dung. They'd spent their early years shoveling piles of dung out of the dragon kennels, day in and day out. "This brings back fond memories."

Dyphestive nodded.

Streak flew into the cave, landed, then crawled over to the pile. "Poop. What a find! Fresh too. I'd say a day old, no more." He loudly sniffed. "Definitely not dragon poop."

"We've assessed that, thank you," Grey Cloak replied. "It's refreshing to know that we are all experts on dung. Streak, you wouldn't happen to have seen any two-headed men who could have created this oversized pile waltzing across these hills?"

"Nope. But I did see a mountain bison. Two of them, in fact." The ends of Streak's tails drummed on the ground in alternating fashion. "And a bobcat. Big ears on that one." He started to wander around the cave. "Did you see these bones?"

There were a lot of human-sized bones scattered around, but they'd also found abandoned weapons and pieces of armor in the cave.

"A lot of people were brought inside here and eaten," Dyphestive said. "It must have been the ettin."

Grey Cloak crouched and picked up a skull. It wasn't very big. It could have been a woman, a child, or even a halfling. Butterflies of guilt fluttered in his stomach. "Unfortunate. It appears this ettin has a merciless appetite. The sooner we kill it, the better." He stood. "Let the hunt resume."

"Glad you understand," said Dyphestive.

"Anything to move away from this stink."

Clumps of snow started to fall over the mouth of the cave. The ground tremored beneath their feet.

"Everyone, get out of here!" Grey Cloak ordered.

The cave rumbled. Boulders and huge hunks of snow rained down over the mouth of the cave, filling the opening and blocking it. In a few moments, the entire entrance was sealed shut. The shaking ground settled.

"Avalanche!" Streak hollered. "That's what you are supposed to say. 'Avalanche.'" He wandered over to the snow blockage. "It won't be easy to dig ourselves out of here. It will take days, if not weeks." He quickly tilted his head like a bird. "Wait, what is that? I hear something on the other side."

Grey Cloak and Dyphestive joined the dragon. Grey Cloak cupped his pointed ear, closed his eyes, and heard a pair of gruff voices laughing.

"Perhaps we underestimated the ettin." Dyphestive dug into the snow. "You know how they say 'Two heads are better than one'?"

"They do say that," Streak said with a nod. "Good one."

Dyphestive carried a handful of snow to the pile of dung and started to cover it. "That ought to help."

Grey Cloak didn't pay his brother any mind. He sat slumped against the cave wall with the cloak covering his nose, studying a small scroll that Tatiana had given him underneath the light of the rod. He simmered inside. Not only did he not want to chase the ettin, but the ettin had managed to dupe them and bury them alive. His brow furrowed as he read the parchment, a list of potions, hoping to find anything useful at all.

"What if we have to eat each other?" Streak asked. "What order would we go in? I know I'm the smallest, but I have to warn you, I'm going to put up a fight."

"No one's going to eat anybody," Grey Cloak said.

"We shouldn't assume anything," Streak continued. "I supposed we could draw straws, but for the cause of the greater good, I believe I should be the last to go. First, I have fire, so it will be a lot easier for me to cook food, and I can eat you both raw. No disrespect. Second, I can hibernate for a very long time, increasing my chances of survival immensely. Please, take no offense. As I said, it's for the greater good."

Dyphestive dropped another pile of snow onto the

dung. "It's a good plan. You are smaller and would be able to feed on us longer than we could feed on you."

Streak nodded. "That's exactly what I mean. I'm glad you get me, Dyphestive."

"No one is eating anyone." Grey Cloak rose with a potion vial clenched in his fist. "I have a way out."

48

DYPHESTIVE TOOK the slender potion vial in the palm of his hand and inspected its cork top and ivy-green wax seal. He pushed the cork off with his thumb and sniffed the contents. His nose twitched. "It smells like that dung over there."

"You aren't supposed to smell it—you're supposed to drink it. So drink up," insisted Grey Cloak.

"What does it do?"

"It's called *Giantus*. It will make you bigger."

With an upward glance, Dyphestive checked the height of the ceiling. "How big will it make me?"

"I don't know. The scroll didn't specify." Grey Cloak gave an impatient snort. "If you won't drink it, I will."

"I'll do it. I want to be big again," Streak said.

"No, I'll do it. Do I drink all of it?"

"I don't know. I assume so. The bigger, the better."

Dyphestive shrugged. "Stand back." He put the vial to his lips. "Bottoms up." He drank. The contents burned like a spicy sauce on the way down. He rubbed his belly. "I feel gummy inside."

Grey Cloak backed away.

His brother belched. He grew a foot. He belched again and started to double in size.

Grey Cloak's own eyes grew. "It's working! Keep belching!"

In a matter of moments, Dyphestive transformed from a big man into a huge giant, his head touching the top of the cave ceiling. "Now what?" he asked in a booming voice.

Grey Cloak motioned toward the snow pile that sealed them in. "Well, dig us out, anvil-head!"

Dyphestive stuffed his humongous hands into the snowy depths and started shoveling.

"Don't bury us!" Grey Cloak said as he shook the snow from his cloak.

"Sorry. I think I have a better approach." Dyphestive got down on all fours, dug his boots into the cave floor, and started plowing forward. The wall of snow heaved outward. He pushed through the huge pile of rock and ice as if it was made out of straw. He bulled his way through to the other side, leaving a clear path behind him. "What are you waiting for? Come on out."

Grey Cloak towed the sled behind him with Streak

riding on top. He smiled. "Well done. I knew I'd think of something."

Dyphestive wiped the snow out of his hair and from his shoulders and rose to full height. He studied his hands and looked at his friends. "I'm huge!" he said in a loud voice. "I like it. How long do you think I'll be this size?"

"I don't know. I'm sure it will wear off eventually, but please, don't leave any giant piles anywhere. That's disgusting."

The ground quaked.

Thooom! The ettin appeared on the high ground. The two-headed monster was covered in wooly white hair from head to toe and was built like an ape. He beat his chest with fists that sounded like thunder. Both heads let out a savage howl. It coiled its legs underneath it then leapt into Dyphestive.

"Ooof!" Dyphestive caught the full weight of the ettin on his chest, and they tumbled down the hillside as one. In a tangle of limbs and hammering fists, they beat each other like war drums. They crashed through some trees and rolled over others. Rocks and hard ledges speared their backs.

The ettin screamed in Dyphestive's face, "Diiieee!" He hit Dyphestive in the jaw with a fist as hard as stone, pumping a fist into his ribs and raking strong fingernails at his eyes. "You are the next meal of White Ice!"

Dyphestive took a beating. The ettin fought like a wild

animal with two larger brains. Everywhere it hit him hurt. Somehow, he twisted under it, set one foot in its gut, and thrust it off.

The ettin crashed into the trees then popped back up with a stunned look, knitting together the eyebrows on its very human faces. "We are White Ice," the right head said.

"We will devour you!" said the head on the left. "Big one!"

Dyphestive got his legs underneath him and managed to stand. *I won't be big forever. Better make the most of it.* He brushed the snow from his chest. "Let's try this dance again, Ugly."

The ettin roared and came at him like a charging bull. He scooped Dyphestive up, hooked his leg, and slammed him to the ground.

Dyphestive cursed. "Horseshoes!" The ettin didn't fight like a normal man—it fought like a wild animal with unpredictable skills. He threw an elbow into its jaw and punched with the other arm.

The ettin shrugged it off like a slap in the face.

They stood toe to toe, exchanging thunderous blows.

Pow! Crack! Boom!

The ettin got the best of him with its savage speed and raw power. Dyphestive's face was bleeding.

"We can taste your blood!" the ettin cried. "We'll gnaw on your bones tonight."

Dyphestive's anger started to boil over the moment the

ettin spoke. He thought of all the innocent blood that had been spilled by the powerful creature. He took another punch to the jaw, standing his ground. "No, you won't."

White Ice attacked. He came in low and hammered Dyphestive's ribs with his fists.

Dyphestive grabbed the long white hairs on White Ice's heads and started slamming the two skulls together. He headbutted one in the face over and over again. His mind was set, and he focused on punishing the head on the left, beating it to a pulp, knocking teeth loose, and pulling out hair. Finally, he landed an uppercut to the left head's jaw.

The ettin's body staggered. The right head roared at the sky and came face-to-face with Streak.

The runt dragon set the right head on fire.

White Ice screamed then started to turn and run.

Dyphestive tackled the back legs. He found a boulder in the snow and busted the left head's skull. He jumped on the ettin's back, put both heads in an armlock, and squeezed. He howled like a savage as mounds of muscle bulged in his arms. He heaved until the ettin's neck bones popped.

49

BACK TO HIS NORMAL SIZE, a battered and bruised Dyphestive rolled one of the ettin's heads into the lumberjack camp, to the shock and amazement of the lumberjack onlookers. Word of White Ice's death spread like wildfire after that, and the camps were turned into gatherings of sheer jubilation.

Hannibull puffed on his pipe. "I can't believe my eyes." He stood by the ettin's head, which was taller than he was. "White Ice is dead. I never thought that day would come. You will always be welcome in our camps."

Grey Cloak tapped his fingers together. "You mentioned that the merchants would be relieved. Tell me more about them."

"You want to contact the Culpepper family. They won't be difficult to find in the township. I'll write you a script so they'll know who you are and what you did." Hannibull punched the ettin's head in the nose. "Always wanted to do that. Hah!" He put his fists on his hips and leaned back. "Grey Cloak and Dyphestive, Legends of the Ridges. Come, let's eat! Let's drink!"

They stayed through the night and headed west early the next day. The swelling and bruising in Dyphestive's face had begun to clear, and he wore a satisfied look on his face while he used a toothpick and pulled the small sled.

"You appear to be awfully pleased with yourself," Grey Cloak said.

"I am. And you should be pleased as well. We potentially saved a lot of lives. And I turned into a giant and killed an ettin."

"We did the right thing, and I'm glad it turned out in our favor." Grey Cloak wiggled his shoulders. "Is everything well back there?"

Streak popped his head out of the hood and rested his neck over Grey Cloak's shoulder. "I sleep like a baby inside the hood. I don't know why, but it's cozy." His tongue flickered, and he stared forward. "Are we there yet?"

"A couple more days of walking, I believe," Grey Cloak replied.

"I'll resume my slumber time. Just wiggle if you need me." Streak nestled back inside the hood.

The brothers walked along the snowy trails day and night, only stopping to eat. They arrived a league away from Ice Vale's township around midday. The sprawling town was surrounded by ice lakes and fields of winter pines.

From a distance, Grey Cloak could make out castles built out of timbers and stone, which reminded him of his time in Loose Boot. On the surrounding hills and in the valley were small cabins and cottages with smoke rolling out of the chimneys. Clusters of men bundled in winter clothing fished through the holes in the ice.

The city in the ice had a warmth about it that drew them toward the township. The people they passed along the roads walked or rode on horse-drawn sleighs and would wave and offer polite salutations.

"It doesn't appear that the world has ended yet," Grey Cloak said. He wiggled his hood, and Streak popped out. "Stay out of sight. I don't want to go through anything like what happened in Loose Boot."

Streak replied, "No problem at all." He tasted the falling snowflakes with his tongue. "This smells like a nice place. Wake me when dinner is ready."

The Ice Vale township dwarfed Loose Boot. It was one of the bigger cities Grey Cloak had ever seen. A network of buildings with steep, high-angled roofs was tightly knit together, all of the porches linked together with a connecting series of walkways. There were gardens of ice sculptures and bonfires at every intersection. Urns of fire burned on every corner.

"I suppose we need to find a place to stay." Grey Cloak spied a tavern with a wide staircase leading to the entrance. "Let's try that one."

At the base of the steps, they were stopped by a man who jumped in front of them. He wore a sea-blue scarf around his neck and a matching long coat. The ferret-looking man's hair was thinning, his eyes beady. "You are Grey Cloak and Dyphestive, are you not?"

They didn't answer.

"The slayers of White Ice? Yes!" he said in an enticing manner. "I am Lorry. I represent the Culpepper family. They would be delighted to meet with you. Immediately." His shifty eyes looked them both over. "You have a letter for me, yes? From Hannibull, yes?"

Grey Cloak removed the parchment from his pocket. "How did you know that?"

Lorry twirled his finger toward the sky and pointed at the birds nesting along the rooftops. "Snow pigeons. We received the good news a day ago." He leaned over and squeezed Dyphestive's arm. "A mighty warrior. Big. Strong. The Culpeppers will like you." He made a fist. "Big. Strong."

Grey Cloak and Dyphestive exchanged suspicious looks while Lorry unwrapped the parchment and read it.

"Yes. Yes. This is very good. A proper confirmation of your identity." Lorry bowed to each of them. "Please allow me to escort you to the Culpepper homestead. You will eat well. You will feel well. You can rest your weary limbs and clean yourselves. The homestead is fantastic. You will see."

Grey Cloak scratched behind his ear. "Lorry, would you share with us what year it is?"

"An odd question, very odd, but Hannibull mentioned that you would inquire about it." He turned his nose to one side and snorted a pinch of snuff. "But who am I to deny such heroes? It is the second season of the year six thousand twelve. Might I ask why you ask?"

Grey Cloak backhanded Dyphestive in the arm. "We're back where we started."

Streak popped his head out of the hood. "Uh oh, it looks like we have to go back to the future."

50

EPILOGUE/DARK MOUNTAIN

THE ZIGGURAT that made up Black Frost's temple had a hollow core that appeared as enormous on the inside as it was on the outside. The main supports were built using slabs of solid granite that formed archways and columns. There were over twenty levels from top to bottom, overlooking the hot lava core at the bottom of the black mountainside it rested upon.

Datris led Gossamer down the stairs from the upper platform, talking the entire way. "I might have the strongest legs in all of Dark Mountain," the soft-spoken elf said. "I ascend and descend the stairs several times a week. But I'm fortunate that Black Frost trusts me to do his bidding on the inside and not outside. The stairs are very slippery, and many have fallen to their deaths."

"I know I almost did." Gossamer leaned over the ledge,

marveling at the strange world below. He could see the pointed rooftops of many chambers built around the lava stream. Huge veins of energy pulsated there, starting from the floor, rising along the walls like silver snakes, and feeding into the top. "What are those?"

"There is much that I need to show you, since we will be working together. Assuming that you are being honest about the information you shared with the Glorious One."

"We'll be working together?"

"Of course. Black Frost has grand plans. He uses people with our skills as foot soldiers. If you please him, you'll be well rewarded. I assure you of that."

Gossamer nodded. "Is your reward walking the stairs night and day?"

"As I said, I now have the strongest legs in the Black Hills." Datris offered an impish smile, and his green eyes sparkled. "If I move too fast, let me know. I'm sure you are weak from the journey to the top of the temple."

"I wouldn't mind resting, but all in due time." Gossamer ambled after Datris, who moved at a steady, graceful pace. He felt ancient and exhausted compared to the young elf. He had been young once but was far older than he appeared, at least until the underlings drained him. The battle with the hydras and opening the portal had taken everything out of him, and then he had to climb the stairs. Walking down them was much easier, and he was relieved when they reached floor level and entered the lower chambers.

"We're almost there. You'll be able to lie down and rest, assuming that you are honest." Datris led him through large corridors walled in with polished stones. "The time with the Tormentors will be over quickly, so long as you are truthful."

They passed an archway with light pouring out that gleamed like the sun.

Gossamer stopped and took a look. A bright circular ring created the edge surrounding a portal to another world. It fed the streams of energy that crawled along the insides of the ziggurat. Leagues of dying fields could be seen on the other side, and then the picture changed. Rivers ran dry. Fish gulped for water. Marvelous civilizations were in decay. "How did this come to be?"

"The portal appeared long ago," Datris answered. "The Wizard Watch tapped into it before it closed, and they were able to keep it open. Black Frost feeds on the abundant life in that world."

"How can this be? I've never heard of this."

"Of course not. The wizards who constructed this are long dead. Black Frost had them killed. That is how he keeps his secrets." Datris tugged on Gossamer's arm. "Come along. We can't delay."

Something else caught his eye—two life-sized statues faced the portal. One was a Herculean man and the other a beautiful elf, both frozen in action. Anguish marred their faces. The man appeared to be clutching a sword that was no longer there. The woman's fingers were empty. "Who are they?"

"That is Olgstern Stronghair and Zanna Paydark. They are the only ones who ever came close enough to close the portal."

"What happened?" Gossamer asked.

"Black Frost, in his wisdom, set a trap and turned them into stone." Datris pulled Gossamer out of the chamber. "We must go. You need to be prepared for your new life."

"I'm surprised that you have shared this information with me. I'm thankful to be enlightened."

In his own warm but impersonal manner, Datris said, "It is of no consequence. The Tormentors will reveal whose side you are really on. If your words are true, there is nothing to fear. If you spoke a lie, it will be your time to walk an eternity behind the flaming fence, courtesy of Black Frost. Here we are."

They entered a dark chamber with pitch-black walls and brass sconces holding flickering flames of amber light. A rectangular platform in the middle of the circular room was cut from a slab of green marble. It sat upon a tank of milky water.

"Lie down on the table, please," Datris said as he closed the curtains to the entrance.

Gossamer did as he was told. His heart started to pound

inside his chest. Fleshy purple tentacles slipped out of the tank of water and seized his arms, legs, and neck. He choked. "Gack!"

A purple-and-black creature with yellow eyes appeared on the slab between his feet. It looked like an octopus but was the size of a pumpkin, and fathomless intelligence lurked in its eyes. The slimy dripping thing crawled over his belly then onto his chest, finally fastening itself to the top of Gossamer's head.

He felt it nod and fought the urge to scream as a dark presence entered his mind and took a strong hold. Its heartbeat pulsed inside his skull.

Datris stood over top of him. "You told Black Frost that you sent Grey Cloak and Dyphestive through the portal into another world. He didn't believe you. I didn't, either. Tell us, where did you send them?"

Gossamer had a strong feeling that he would be killed instantly if he lied. He didn't want to battle the monster sucking on his head, so he opted for the truth and took a leap of faith. "I lied. I didn't send them to another world. I sent them to the past."

"Interesting. You tell the truth, or your mind would be food right now. How far in the past?"

"As far as I had the strength to send them. Several years, perhaps."

"Again, you don't lie." Datris tapped his index finger on

his chin. "One more question. Are you trying to stop Black Frost?"

"No. I'm trying to destroy him."

Datris nodded. "You tell the truth again. Interesting."

With Grey Cloak and Dyphestive trapped in the past, how will they save the future?

Whose side is Gossamer really on?

And where in the world did the Iron Sword come from?

Don't forget to leave a review for Grey Cloak: Dragon Wars - Book 13. They are a huge help! LINK!

Learn more about the world of BISH in my other Sword and Sorcery Masterpiece, The Darkslayer Omnibus!

If you want to learn more about Commander Slaught and Fredrake, be sure that you don't miss the prequel to Dragon Wars. HERE IS THE FREE LINK!

Grab your copy of *Barbarian Backlash – Book 14*, On Sale Now! Click here! See pic below.

And if you haven't already, signup for my newsletter and grab 3 FREE books including the Dragon Wars Prequel.

WWW.DRAGONWARSBOOKS.COM

Teachers and Students, if you would like to order paperback copies for you library or classroom, email craig@thedarkslayer.com to receive a special discount.

Gear up in this Dragon Wars body armor enchanted with a +2 Coolness factor/+4 at Gaming Conventions. Sizes range from halfling (Small) to Ogre (XXL). LINK . www.society6.com

ABOUT THE AUTHOR

Please leave a review. They are a huge help to me! Post a review, email me the link, and I'll send you a free copy of Book Two. Here is a link.

*Check me out on Bookbub and follow HalloranOn-BookBub

*I'd love it if you would subscribe to my mailing list: www.craighalloran.com

*On Facebook, you can find me at The Darkslayer Report or Craig Halloran.

*Twitter, Twitter, Twitter. I am there too: www.twitter.com/CraigHalloran

*And of course, you can always email me at craig@thedarkslayer.com

See my book lists below!

OTHER BOOKS

Craig Halloran resides with his family outside his hometown of Charleston, West Virginia. When he isn't entertaining mankind, he is seeking adventure, working out, or watching sports. To learn more about him, go to www.thedarkslayer.com.

Check out all my great stories...

Free Books

> The Darkslayer: Brutal Beginnings
> Nath Dragon—Quest for the Thunderstone

The Chronicles of Dragon Series 1 (10-book series)

> The Hero, the Sword and the Dragons (Book 1)
> Dragon Bones and Tombstones (Book 2)

Terror at the Temple (Book 3)

Clutch of the Cleric (Book 4)

Hunt for the Hero (Book 5)

Siege at the Settlements (Book 6)

Strife in the Sky (Book 7)

Fight and the Fury (Book 8)

War in the Winds (Book 9)

Finale (Book 10)

Boxset 1-5

Boxset 6-10

Collector's Edition 1-10

Tail of the Dragon, The Chronicles of Dragon, Series 2 (10-book series)

Tail of the Dragon #1

Claws of the Dragon #2

Battle of the Dragon #3

Eyes of the Dragon #4

Flight of the Dragon #5

Trial of the Dragon #6

Judgement of the Dragon #7

Wrath of the Dragon #8

Power of the Dragon #9

Hour of the Dragon #10

Boxset 1-5

Boxset 6-10

Collector's Edition 1-10

The Odyssey of Nath Dragon Series (New Series) (Prequel to Chronicles of Dragon)

Exiled

Enslaved

Deadly

Hunted

Strife

The Darkslayer Series 1 (6-book series)

Wrath of the Royals (Book 1)

Blades in the Night (Book 2)

Underling Revenge (Book 3)

Danger and the Druid (Book 4)

Outrage in the Outlands (Book 5)

Chaos at the Castle (Book 6)

Boxset 1-3

Boxset 4-6

Omnibus 1-6

The Darkslayer: Bish and Bone, Series 2 (10-book series)

Bish and Bone (Book 1)

Black Blood (Book 2)

Red Death (Book 3)

Lethal Liaisons (Book 4)

Torment and Terror (Book 5)

Brigands and Badlands (Book 6)

War in the Wasteland (Book 7)

Slaughter in the Streets (Book 8)

Hunt of the Beast (Book 9)

The Battle for Bone (Book 10)

Boxset 1-5

Boxset 6-10

Bish and Bone Omnibus (Books 1-10)

CLASH OF HEROES: Nath Dragon meets The Darkslayer mini series

Book 1

Book 2

Book 3

The Henchmen Chronicles

The King's Henchmen

The King's Assassin

The King's Prisoner

The King's Conjurer

The King's Enemies

The King's Spies

The Gamma Earth Cycle

Escape from the Dominion

Flight from the Dominion

Prison of the Dominion

The Supernatural Bounty Hunter Files (10-book series)

Smoke Rising: Book 1

I Smell Smoke: Book 2

Where There's Smoke: Book 3

Smoke on the Water: Book 4

Smoke and Mirrors: Book 5

Up in Smoke: Book 6

Smoke Signals: Book 7

Holy Smoke: Book 8

Smoke Happens: Book 9

Smoke Out: Book 10

Boxset 1-5

Boxset 6-10

Collector's Edition 1-10

Zombie Impact Series

Zombie Day Care: Book 1

Zombie Rehab: Book 2

Zombie Warfare: Book 3

Boxset: Books 1-3

OTHER WORKS & NOVELLAS

The Red Citadel and the Sorcerer's Power